CRITICAL

Jane Adams

The Greenway

Cast the First Stone

'Adams's debut last year, *The Greenway*, hinted at a promising crime-writing talent; *Cast the First Stone* amply confirms that view.' Marcel Berlins, *The Times*

'A powerful and corrosive thriller about child abuse, suspicion and guilt. Gripping, scary, a wonderful read. She could rise to the top of the genre.' *Yorkshire Post*

'The grippingly edgy quality of this *policier* . . . is taut-ened almost unbearably.' *Sunday Times*

'Will keep you on the edge of your seat from the first few pages until the chilling climax.' *Stirling Observer*

Bird

'Jane Adams' first two novels of psychological suspense promised a major talent in the making. With *Bird* she amply fulfils that promise with assurance and style.' Val McDermid, *Manchester Evening News*

'The art of the truly great suspense novel, an art which Adams has mastered.' *Crime Time*

'I am a great fan of good commercial fiction, and it rarely comes better than Jane Adams' *Bird*. It is a haunting crime novel and psychodrama pulling all the right strings in all the right places.' *The Bookseller*

Fade to Grey

'A cleverly constructed, slow-to-unravel crime mystery, the third in the DI Mike Croft series.' *South Wales Argus*

'An intriguing thriller ... A good suspense story.' *Caithness Courier*

Fade to Grey

Jane Adams was born in Leicester, where she still lives. She has a degree in sociology, and has held a variety of jobs including lead vocalist in a folk rock band. She enjoys pen and ink drawing, two martial arts (Aikido and Tae Kwon Do) and her ambition is to travel the length of the Silk Road by motorbike. She is married with two children.

Fade to Grey is the third novel in the series featuring Detective Inspector Mike Croft, following *The Greenway* and *Cast the First Stone*. In 1995 *The Greenway*, her debut novel, was nominated both for the Crime Writers' Association John Creasey Award for best first crime novel of 1995 and the Author's Club Best First Novel award. Jane's latest novel, *Final Frame*, is a direct sequel to *Fade to Grey* and is available in hardback from Macmillan.

Jane Adams is also the author of *Bird*, a chilling ghost story now available in Pan Books.

Fade to Grey

Jane Adams

PAN BOOKS

First published 1998 by Macmillan

This edition published 1999 by Pan Books
an imprint of Macmillan Publishers Ltd
25 Eccleston Place, London SW1W 9NF
Basingstoke and Oxford
Associated companies throughout the world
www.macmillan.com

ISBN 0 330 37487 7

Phototypeset by Intype London Ltd
Printed and bound in Great Britain
Mackays of Chatham plc, Chatham, Kent

For Shaun – 'The Pit Crew' – for his unfailing enthusiasm. Bless you.

And for Stuart. Above and beyond the call . . .

Thanks, Peter!

Right now: I do not want to be told truth.
I want lies. Sweetly spoken:
Courteously deformed,
Deferring to my need for compliment.

Right now, I need ...
No. Not even words.
I want the lies the body tells,
The caress of flesh
Warm arms curved tight
And a soft touch – though not so soft,
> *My soul*
> *Cannot feel it burn.*

Right now:
I do not want the demon lover:
Or the secret longings
> *Which call my name from the deepest shadows,*
I want only ... lies ...
> *Sweet and sensual lies ...*
Easing me into peace.

Or make them truths
> *If you so desire*

But tell me nothing,
> *That ...*
> *I do not need ...*
> *To hear.*

Prologue

She took a good photograph, anyone would say so. She had that look about her, that little bit of self-doubt, or not quite innocence, that men found so appealing. Some men.

She'd always resisted Jake's attempts to make her look even younger than she was. The schoolgirl look or the baby doll just wasn't her style, she said. Though it was amazing what you could do with the right software package these days.

In the end he'd turned her out pretty much any way he wanted and she hadn't said a word about it.

He turned the pages of the latest magazine. Computer porn might be the newest thing, but personally he preferred the finished article to be one he could roll up and carry in his pocket.

Which he did now, tucking the magazine into the inside pocket of his coat.

It would be a collector's item before long, this edition. In certain circles anyway. Those that were in the know . . .

Not because it was anything harder than you could pick up from the top shelf of any news-stand. Nothing more than soft porn in this edition. The other stuff, the stuff he could have been arrested for if he'd been caught prancing round town with it, that was elsewhere. Already distributed on the multimedia wave.

No, it wasn't the content that made this little package rare, but the scarcity of the commodity.

There would be no more centrefolds of this little lady. Not unless, of course, you liked your meat well done . . .

Thursday,
15 December

Chapter One

Norwich 6.05 p.m.

Stacey hesitated before squeezing through the gap next to the park gates. It was dark in there but it was also the quickest way of getting home. Besides, turning around and walking back the way she'd come would mean running into Richard again and she just knew he'd be standing around, waiting for her to come back to him. Well, sod that! Stacey wasn't going to apologize for anything. Let him stew for a while.

Once inside the park she stopped and groped in her bag for the little penlight torch she had attached to her key-ring. The thin beam of light showed her only a few yards of the muddy path before it was swallowed by the thick darkness. She slid her finger through the ring, posting the key in between her fingers the way that guy in the self-defence class had told them to. Nervous now, her mind niggling about those reports in the papers.

Maybe after all she should go back and find Richard. Not apologize exactly, just open the discussion enough for him to give her a ride home.

She glanced back over her shoulder one more time, startled by what sounded like a footstep.

'Richard? Is that you?' No reply. 'Richard. Oh for Christ's sake, if that's you . . .'

She shone the torch back through the wrought-iron

gates but could see nothing, no one at all walking along the lonely street.

Stacey moved swiftly down what she could see of the slimy, leaf-covered path. The silence seemed to close in all around her, only the heels of her boots clacking with a reassuringly steady beat as she walked and the jingle of loose change in her pocket breaking the quiet.

Stacey shivered. It had begun to rain and the air was damp and clammy against her skin. Thinking she would be driven home, she had worn her denim jacket and left her umbrella on the table in the hall. She quickened her pace now as the rain fell more heavily.

And then it happened, footsteps, the sound of someone running making her look back. Richard's name half spoken before one hand was clamped around her mouth and a second hand grabbing at her breasts, the man's body pressed tight against her back. Then he shifted sideways and she was on the floor even before she realized that she was falling. The hand gone from her mouth now, Stacey screamed in fear, then in pain as the fist came crashing down at the side of her head.

Only half-conscious, she still tried to wriggle away from him. Felt the sudden chill of air on her legs and stomach as he wrenched her skirt up above her waist. Hard fingers bruising as they grabbed between her legs.

Stacey tried to scream again, but he was on top of her, his body heavy on her chest and his breath hot in her face. He was saying something but Stacey was too stunned to understand the words.

The torch, the keys, somehow she had managed to keep hold of them, the ring still tight around her finger.

She brought her right hand up, striking into the man's face. Her left hand reaching and grabbing at his hair, winding her fingers tight and pulling as hard as she could. Adrenalin and fear had overcome the pain of her bruised and bleeding head and half-closed eye.

The man was yelling now, loosening his grip on her just for an instant. Stacey hit out at him again, fighting for her life as he came back at her, his hands tightening on her throat.

Norwich 7 p.m.

Mike sat uneasily between Maria and her sister Josie, watching as three wise men, bearing gold-wrapped boxes, slow-marched across the stage. Enthusiastic music, played on a slightly off-key piano, helped to keep them in time, left feet, right feet, lifted in unison like an odd, dissociated caterpillar making its way towards the manger.

He tried desperately not to fidget. The hard plastic of the chair was digging into his back and there was no room to stretch out his long legs. A tall man who liked space to move around, Mike felt over-large and over-conspicuous wedged in between proud parents and grandparents. His body cramped and his mind over-whelmed by remembrance of another time when his son Stevie had been one of the three kings. Wearing his father's old plaid dressing-gown and holding his gift high as he presented it to the little girl cuddling the baby doll.

'Doesn't she look lovely?'

It was Maria, smiling happily at her niece. Little Essie was grinning so much she almost forgot her words. Her thick black hair, braided tightly and threaded with blue and yellow beads, swung around her face as she strutted forward with her arms outstretched to take the presents from the kings. Mike didn't have to look sideways to know that Josie dabbed at tears watching her little girl up on the stage.

He tried hard to smile, knowing he should feel grateful to be included in such a family time, but it brought back so many morbid thoughts; since Stevie had died, he'd always found it hard to cope with this pre-Christmas rush of emotion.

The angels were just about to break into a new song when the beeping started, breaking into the giggling hush of children too small to be really quiet. Mike grabbed at his pocket to silence it, aware of Maria's glare as he peeked a look at the number on the LCD screen. He unfolded himself awkwardly from the little plastic chair, trying hard not to catch her eye as he headed for the door, apologizing as he went and horribly conscious of every inch of his six-foot-two frame.

Maria caught up with him at the outer door.

'I thought I told you to leave that bloody thing behind.'

'Well, no, actually it was the phone you told me to leave behind . . .' He smiled sheepishly. 'It's work,' he said.

'Isn't it always?'

'Um, I need the car keys, the phone . . .'

She sighed in exasperation and dug into her pocket

for the keys. 'You'd better take the car,' she said. 'I'll get a lift back with Josie.'

'Thanks.' He paused, wondering if he should risk a kiss goodbye. He reached out and caught her hand instead.

'I'm really sorry.'

'You're always really sorry.' Maria shook her head. 'God! Never get yourself involved with a policeman.'

He watched her as she stalked away, shoulders set, irritation flowing from every pore. This was the third time in as many already scarce evenings off that he'd been called away. He could understand her getting mad at him. Mike was relieved when she glanced back from the door, not quite smiling, but her expression softening enough to let him know he was off the hook . . . almost.

Then he got into the car, rummaged in the glove compartment for the phone and called the office. 'DI Mike Croft.' He listened in silence as they told him about the latest attack.

'They've taken her to the Royal and District, Mike. Price is interviewing the boyfriend.'

'Is she badly hurt?'

'Bruising, shock. They'll be keeping her overnight though. You'll want to speak to the boyfriend?'

Mike signed off and turned the ignition key, listening to the low purr of the engine for a moment or two before pulling away. His mind already cataloguing the new information, he turned the car towards the hospital.

Chapter Two

West Kennet, Wiltshire 7 p.m.

The light drizzle had begun when the old man left the house, walking the dogs out of Avebury village and across on the straight route to the Devizes road. It was already dark, and the mist and rain cut visibility even further. To his left the ridge of West Kennet long barrow rose from the downs, and the cone of Silbury Hill loomed out of the mist in front of him. He could barely make out either familiar landmark through the dark and rain that fell more determinedly minute by minute. And it was turning uncomfortably cold. He decided that he and the dogs were getting too old to be traipsing about in this kind of weather. That he should cut the evening walk short and head for home.

As he turned, a red glow caught his eye. He peered through the grey murk trying to make sense of it and as he did the redness grew larger, flowering more brightly against the backdrop of grey.

'What the . . .' He took a few steps across the road and started along the path that led up the ridge towards the barrow. The blaze had full hold now and as he drew closer he realized that what he was seeing was a car, flames and thick black smoke billowing out of a part-open window.

'Bloody joy-riders.' He watched enough television to know the latest trends in crime.

But he was curious about the car and, thinking about it, more than a little confused. Surely if joy-riders had set the vehicle alight he should have seen them running away. Seen something, even through the filthy rain doing its best to penetrate his topcoat. It would have made most sense for them to have run back towards the road, towards him and the dogs and away from the fire. Go the other way and they'd have to scramble over fences into the fields beyond.

Leaning heavily on his stick, not certain whether he should beat a hasty retreat – who could tell what kind of young hooligan stole cars and then set fire to them? – or go further up the track and see if he could make out which way the miscreants had run, the old man took a few hesitant steps forward. He circled wide of the burning car, knowing that the petrol tank could blow at any time.

'Oh my sweet Lord,' he whispered, 'Oh my Lord,' as the black plumes of smoke parted just for an instant and he could see through the open window a slumped figure in the driver's seat of the blazing car.

Chapter Three

Hoton, Norwich 8.15 p.m.

John Tynan sipped his tea and stared absently at the television set. He often wondered why he watched television police dramas. They were usually so far removed from anything he'd ever been involved with while he was on the force, and their ignorance of procedure often made him cringe. Still, he enjoyed them all the same.

This was better than most, he thought. Good characters, so he could forgive the inaccuracy. And he was pretty certain he knew who'd done it.

Tynan leaned forward to get himself more tea, watching the screen as he eased the blue and yellow knitted cosy from the brown pot, following the two major characters as they poked around in the aftermath of a house fire.

'Damn and blast!' The insistent ringing of the doorbell broke across his concentration. 'Who the hell . . . at this time of night?'

Reluctantly, John Tynan made his way across the overcrowded little room and out into the hall, wrenching the front door open with an impatient tug.

'Hello, John.'

'Maria!' He stared in surprise at the tall black woman standing on his doorstep. 'Come in, come in.'

Maria turned to wave her hand towards a waiting car, then stepped into Tynan's hallway. 'Oh, but it's cold out there. Josie just dropped me off,' she said, explaining the car. 'I had to let Mike take my car, only realized after he'd gone that his flat key was on the ring and it's too far to get back to Oaklands tonight.' She turned to kiss John swiftly on the cheek. 'Hope you don't mind?'

'Mind? No. Welcome as spring, my dear. But hurry in, I'm watching that police thing on TV and he's just about to get it all wrong again.'

Maria laughed and followed John through to the living-room, unbuttoning her coat and unknotting the green silk scarf she wore at her throat.

'Are you cold? Pull the chair close to the fire, that's it.' John took her coat and laid it on the ottoman that stood near the window, then resumed his place on the two-seater sofa. 'I'll make you some tea in a minute.'

'No hurry, John.' She nodded towards the television. 'Know who did it yet?'

'I'll put money on the husband.' He smiled across at her. 'Mike get called in again?'

'That's right. It's getting to be normal. I don't know, but my guess is it's another assault.'

John nodded in agreement, glancing back at the television to keep up with the plot. 'They seem to be getting nowhere about as fast as this lot do,' he said.

Maria stretched, then got up again. 'Mind if I use your phone?' she asked. 'I'd better leave him a message. Tell him where I am or he'll think I'm really mad with him.'

'Well, help yourself, my dear. I'll see about getting some more tea.'

8.30 p.m.

Mike had spent only a short time at the hospital. Stacey had been able to tell him very little. Concussion and shock, her doctor had said. It would be better to try again in the morning. Mike had agreed. Stacey's mother had arrived by the time he'd left; the parents had been out at a party and it had taken a bit of time to find them. They'd been horrified, devastated that this had happened to their child. At first furious with Stacey's boyfriend, for letting her storm off alone, then, in the same breath, grateful that he'd decided to follow and had saved their daughter.

The front office was empty but for the desk sergeant who buzzed him through. Mike mooched towards his own office, wondering what Maria was doing and if she'd recovered her good mood yet. Used to being on call herself, she was tolerant of the strange hours he often kept but just lately the interruptions had seemed constant.

Sergeant Price was already there, seated behind Mike's desk and sorting through some papers. He looked up with a quick smile as Mike came in.

'Oh, hello there, guv. It's not typed up yet, but I thought you'd want a look first thing. By the way, Maria phoned. Said she's at John Tynan's. Apparently you took her keys.'

'Blast it.' Mike felt in his pocket. 'One more thing wrong tonight.'

He plonked himself down in the chair opposite,

eyeing the paperwork Price had been shuffling. 'What's that?'

'Statement of one Richard Mattheson. Boyfriend of Stacey Holmes, the girl who was attacked.'

'Oh. I've just come from the hospital. Big waste of time that was. Too shocked and too well sedated to get anywhere tonight.'

'I've sent the boyfriend back to the hospital.'

'Oh, so he's already gone?' Mike was a little put out. 'I came in intending to talk to him.'

'Sorry, guv, but he'd already made a full statement and he wanted to get back to his girl. We dragged him over here while forensics did their bit, but it didn't seem right to hang on to him longer than we had to.'

Mike sighed. It had been a wasted evening all round, it seemed. He suddenly felt surplus to requirements and bitter about having lost time with Maria to no purpose.

'The boyfriend. What did he have to say?'

'Briefly, that she'd stormed off after a silly argument. He'd let her stew for a while then followed her.' Price smiled tightly. 'Seems she's the fiery type. He generally gives her a bit of cooling off time before he tries to make peace. Anyway, he got concerned and went after her. Followed her and realized when he reached that dead end near the park gates that she must've gone through. Just gets over the gate and he hears her screaming. The bastard's on top of her by the time lover-boy arrives and drags him off, and of course he's too busy comforting the girl to go chasing after her attacker. Just knows he ran off towards the main path.'

'How long before our people were on the scene?'

'Less than seven minutes. We beat the ambulance. The boyfriend had a mobile, called it straight in. No sign though. It's pitch black in the park that time of night.'

Mike nodded thoughtfully and skimmed through the written statement. 'She fought back?' he asked, picking up on the one thing Price hadn't mentioned.

'Yeah.' The sergeant sounded chuffed at the thought. 'Like the boyfriend said, she's got a temper. She'd got her keys in her hand and hit the bastard at the side of the face with the sharp end. Pity she didn't take his eye out. As it is, he'll hopefully have nice, visible scratches to remember her by. We've told the press office to make a big thing of that. Might shake a few trees.'

Mike nodded. Anything new would be welcome just now, though it was just as likely to result in the exposure of anyone who'd cut themselves shaving that morning.

'Right then,' he said, getting wearily to his feet once more. 'Nothing more to be done tonight.' He paused at the door. 'Eight-thirty at the hospital. They should have breakfast over by then.' He grinned wryly, remembering his own recent stay. He'd returned to full duty only two weeks before and been landed with a serial rapist.

'Sick leave,' Superintendent Flint had told him ironically. 'DI Pike's been handling it but he's off with a hernia. Caseload too heavy for him, no doubt. So I've put it in your in-tray. Time for a fresh eye.'

Making his way down the stairs to the front office, Mike wondered vaguely why he always managed to get landed with the messy ones.

Friday,
16 December

Chapter Four

2 a.m.

Jake had been waiting for close on an hour. He was good at waiting, patient that way. What he needed now was a little luck. The right person to come out and to do it soon before the crowd started to leave en masse. It was always a gamble, when Jake was asked to make something to order like this. However much forward planning he did there was also an element of luck in casting the right person for the role and, sometimes, luck wasn't available for hire. Jake figured he had maybe another fifteen minutes of clear time; after that, the game would not be worth the risk. There would be other nights.

The street was off the main drag; there was little passing trade not headed for the club. By two in the morning even the doormen had retreated inside. Usually, by that time, more people had already been crammed inside than would upset the local fire chief. After that, the doors opened at intervals only to let people out.

That suited Jake. Standing in the shadows, he could see with little risk of being seen and those that occasionally emerged were far too drunk or otherwise involved to take notice.

Jake was about to give up when the right one came out. First, two young men, arms thrown about each other, falling through the door on a raft of music. The one Jake wanted was with them. His blond hair brassy in the street-light, tight shirt and jeans accentuating a lithe body. He stood almost still, pulling on a leather jacket, shivering against the sudden cold.

He was perfect, Jake thought, just perfect.

Jake waited as the three of them went through their farewells, the small ritual, exaggerated by alcohol becoming stumbling pantomime. Jake could hear their laughter from where he stood across the street, invisible and silent until the couple finally helped each other stagger on their way and the one he wanted wandered on alone down the empty street.

Jake waited a little longer, knowing there was no hurry. The sound of the young man's uneven footsteps were audible even when he turned the corner into a side road. Jake followed then, not wanting to be too far from his car. His rubber-soled shoes made little sound on the wet path and he moved without hurrying, not troubling to hide himself now. Anyone looking would just see a man walking as though he had somewhere to go, he wouldn't even get a second look.

Turning the corner, Jake saw the one he wanted right ahead. He was making slow progress, his steps meandering, body swaying slightly as though he had forgotten that he'd left the club and could still hear music. Deliberately, Jake crossed the road, not following now, but seeking to draw level, then a little ahead. His target saw him, glancing his way briefly but seeing only a man who'd stopped and was searching through his pockets to find a cigarette. Glancing across the street, Jake put the cigarette between his lips and patted at his pockets, frowning a little. Then he crossed the road.

"Scuse me, mate, you haven't got a light, have you?'

'Sorry, I don't smoke,' the man shrugged. His words were slightly slurred, then he swayed backwards slightly, taking a step to steady himself. He pointed. 'There's a little shop round there somewhere. Always open. Bet they'd have some.'

'Right, thanks.' Jake took the cigarette from between his lips and put a hand in his coat as though to find the pack. The younger man began to turn away but Jake had fired the tazer before he took another step, and he fell down, gasping, trying to cry out, as 25,000 volts surged through his system, the wire pinned to his body gleaming in the street-light. Then Jake had the hypodermic in his hand and plunged it into his victim's arm.

Bending, he hauled the young man to his feet and pulled a limp arm around his neck. The victim was just about conscious enough to move his feet as Jake half-dragged him along the road. His car was parked only a street away, and Jake didn't hurry; he slurred his foot-steps and his speech, falling off the pavement and stumbling along in the gutter, enjoying the role even though there didn't seem to be anyone to hear.

Then he dumped the now unconscious body into the boot of his car and settled himself in the driver's seat. Jake was smiling as he drove away.

Norwich 2.15 a.m.

The silence of the sleeping house was soothing as he sat alone, television on, sound turned right down.

His face was sore where she'd caught him with the keys and his jaw ached from where the man had thumped him in the mouth.

The physical discomforts, though, they were nothing compared to the piercing anger at having been interrupted.

He had hung around the park afterwards, staying in the shadows just feet away from the police searchers storming their big-footed, cocky way down the narrow maze of paths. One passing so close he could have reached out and tripped him. Watched him break his great fat face falling on to the concrete.

It gave him one hell of a buzz, that. Knowing he was so close and they knew nothing about it. Almost made up for what he'd lost. Almost . . .

Time for another letter, maybe, telling them just what great clumsy fools they'd been.

He'd been disappointed when they hadn't published his letters. Not even mentioned them in any of the reports that he had read or seen on the TV.

It did cause him a moment's worry, that they knew. Knew about him and about the other one. The one who'd started the whole game.

Chapter Five

DCI Charlie Morrow sat at his desk in Devizes HQ with his back to the radiator, steaming gently. It was a filthy night. Charlie was soaked through despite his coat and there had been no sleep and bugger all to eat.

He glanced at the pictures in front of him. The first ones, processed in a hurry and rushed through to him only moments before.

The photographs made the crime scene look like a film set. The bright glare of the dragon lamps and the eerie flaring from the lights of the fire tender heightened contrast and detail. Blackness beyond the rough circle of light and activity, though even the darkness was in turn swallowed up by the mist rolling wetly across the downs.

What the photographs could not show was the cold misery of spending the best part of the night waiting for a bloody car to cool down enough for SOCO to get a proper look.

He pulled the photos of the body closer to him and stared hard at the charred remains. Contorted legs and arms, blackened torso. The whole looking more like a lump of burned carpet than what had, a short time before, been a human being.

The growling of his stomach reminded Charlie that he was hungry. He was also dead tired and not in the best of humours. Impatiently he shoved the photographs into the folder and dumped it on top of the pile of telephone statements. Then he heaved his not inconsiderable bulk out of his chair and ambled towards the door.

The car was stolen, that much they knew; it had gone missing from its owner's drive two nights before. The owner had not been best pleased to find his pride and joy was now not only a burned-out wreck but had a badly fried body in the driver's seat. He'd been even less pleased to be woken at three in the morning to be apprised of the fact.

Charlie lifted his coat from the peg and shrugged into it, shivering slightly at the feel of damp clothes beneath. He really ought to go back and change before the morning's briefing. At least that would give Mickey's place a chance to open and he could fit breakfast in before the hired help arrived. Brightened by the fact that he'd solved at least one of the morning's problems, Charlie Morrow switched out the light and headed for home.

Chapter Six

'Will you need a lift back to town?' Maria asked.

Mike shook his head. 'Thanks, but no. Price is coming out to pick me up; the garage should have finished with my car by midday.'

'Why don't you just give in and part-ex it? Get something like mine.' Maria's new Mazda was her pride and joy.

'He wouldn't get part-ex on a roller skate, the state his old wreck's in,' John began.

'There's nothing wrong with my car . . .'

'That a can of petrol and a lighter wouldn't solve,' Maria put in swiftly. 'Seriously, Mike, it's about as reliable as a burnt match. This is the third time in a month you've had problems with it.'

'I know, I know, but it would be like trading in an old friend.'

'I hope when I get that decrepit you'll have sense enough to give me a decent burial,' John told him. 'You're heading straight to the hospital?' he continued, changing tack.

Mike nodded. 'Said we'd get there early to talk to the girl. And the initial forensics reports should be back this morning.'

A car horn sounded from the narrow road outside

John's cottage. 'That'll be Price.' Mike bent to kiss Maria. 'I'll give you a ring.'

'I must be off too,' she said. 'I'll just give you a hand to tidy up, John. Then back to it, I guess. You're out tonight, aren't you? Your wife's old friend?'

'Yes, Theo Howard. You've got a busy day?'

She nodded. 'Full case load today and some private stuff tonight.' She grinned. 'Got to pay for the car somehow, you know.'

The cottage seemed very empty after Mike and Maria had gone. Tynan finished putting away the breakfast things and then wondered what to do with the rest of his morning.

A small Christmas tree stood in the hall, ready to be trimmed. First time he had bothered in years, since Grace had died in fact. Mike and Maria would be spending the holiday with him this year. Grace had loved this time of year. John was used to being busy and retirement had not come easily. There had been a time, while his wife Grace was alive, when the prospect of time at home without the pressures of police work had been a very attractive one. But Grace had died. Cancer taking her from him. Nothing had ever quite filled the gap.

Tynan wandered into the living-room and switched on the radio. It was still tuned to her favourite station. Tchaikovsky, one of the few composers he could actually recognize, flooded the room with richness. Impatiently, Tynan wiped the blurring of tears from his eyes.

8.00 a.m.

Cavendish Road in Norwich was a quiet street. Ordinary and suburban. A row of what had once been prosperous Victorian villas, complete with basements, lined one side of the road. They were now mostly divided into flats and bedsits. The other side, slightly later and more modest terraces, occupied for the most part by young couples buying their first home.

The street behind Cavendish Road, Sullivan Avenue, still retained its sense of grandeur. Tree-lined, habited by prosperous family houses, Edwardian semis with sweeping bay windows and cramped but well-paved driveways.

At the end of Cavendish Road itself stood a terraced block of five, divided from the rest by an alleyway. Their small rear yards backed on to the gardens of Sullivan Avenue. This was a neat, red brick row, each with a little forecourt, net curtains at the windows and a couple of steps leading up to the front door.

Theo Howard stood on the steps of the end one of these five, clasping her pink towelling robe tightly closed over her half-dressed body as she bent down to collect the morning's milk. Despite the robe, she looked neat and wide awake. Her thick grey hair was already combed and her make-up carefully applied to make the most of her large blue eyes.

She straightened up and took a moment to survey the street before turning back inside. Watching as the milk float trundled its noisy way around the corner.

27

Waving briefly as her neighbour got into his car and left for work.

A few of the older children were already on their way to school, wandering towards the main road to catch their bus. She watched as the boy went by. His dark hair needed cutting again and his trainers, as usual, bore the traces of last night's football game. Theo almost lifted her hand to wave to him, but resisted at the last moment, knowing there would be no response. He was far too aloof to hope for that. Instead she smiled and, clutching the milk bottle with both hands, ducked back inside and closed the door.

Davy was already engrossed in the morning papers.

'More tea?'

'Thanks.'

A lock of dark hair had fallen forward across his forehead, reminding her of the boy, making him look even younger than he was. She flopped down in the chair opposite and reached out for the teapot. Sitting there, his mind absorbed by breakfast and the morning news, Theo could watch him at her leisure. Admire the dark curls and the smooth, clean-shaven face. The way the muscles of his jaw dimpled and the brows creased as something in the paper caught his eye.

Theo shook her head, laughing inwardly at the butterfly feeling in her stomach that happened every time she looked at him. If only, she thought with a deep and wrenching sadness, these moments could go on for ever.

She gave herself a little shake and looked around for distraction from the melancholy that threatened, glancing instead at the headlines on the morning paper.

'Oh!' she exclaimed. 'Aston Park.'

'What?'

'The headlines on the paper,' she pointed them out. 'Another girl. Whatever is it all coming to?'

He nodded. 'You take care tonight. Get a taxi back from night school if you decide not to drive yourself.'

'Oh, I will, I will. Not that anyone's going to bother with an old thing like me.'

She caught Davy's smile from across the table. 'Fishing, Theo?' he asked. Then put the paper down and drained his tea. Even at fifty-two, they both knew that Theo could still turn heads.

'Got to go,' Davy said. 'Take care today. I mean it.'

He came around to her side of the table and kissed her lightly on the cheek, avoiding her lipstick. Then gathered up his coat and briefcase, his mind already on the day ahead.

'What did you do to your face?' Theo asked him. 'You never did get around to telling me.'

'Oh,' he said, touching a finger lightly against his temple. 'Cupboard door at work. Some fool left it open.'

She watched him go, finishing her tea, the pleasure brought by Davy's company dissipating as she thought of her own day.

Sighing, Theo got to her feet and took the pots over to the kitchen sink.

'Oh damn,' she said suddenly, looking out of the window to see if Davy's car had already gone. She'd meant to remind him to be home on time. John Tynan had telephoned the evening before and confirmed, after all, that he'd be coming to dinner.

She reached into the pocket of her robe. Inside was a folded piece of paper covered with neatly written words. It began: 'Right now; I do not need to be told truth.'

The boy with the unruly hair and dirty trainers hesitated at the corner of the road and stared, frowning towards Sullivan Avenue. His frown disappeared as the girl came racing around the corner. She stopped, catching her breath as she got to him and fell into step.

'God, I thought I was going to be late. Trying to get my homework finished. I've been up since six. You done yours?'

Terry shrugged. 'Got the maths done. English doesn't have to be in till tomorrow.' He scuffed his feet. 'I looked for you last night at the recce. Waited till nearly nine.'

'Yeah, I'm sorry,' Sarah told him. 'I did say I didn't think I could get out and my dad was fussing round, looking at my work and stuff. You know how he is.'

'Sure.' He fell silent for a moment, then brightened. 'Still on for Saturday?'

'Course it is. I'm going Christmas shopping with Maddie in the afternoon so I'll be getting changed at her place. We'll go to the party from there.'

'What have you told your parents?'

'That I'm going out with Maddie and the rest of the crowd. I mean it's not really a lie, is it? Most of them will be at the party.'

He shrugged, but said nothing. The bus was coming and they had to run to make it to the stop in time.

From the window of the flat Judith watched her son walk down the street and pause at the corner of the road.

Terry was old enough to get his own breakfast, but she got up and had coffee with him, needing some kind of kick to get her started on her day. She waited till he'd gone to have her first cigarette. She knew it was stupid, but somehow hated him to see her doing anything that she felt was slightly wrong. He'd had such a rough time, been away from her so long . . .

Sighing, Judith moved away from the window. She made herself a second cup of coffee, took it and her early morning cigarette into the bedroom and turned on the radio. She listened with half an ear to the morning news as she smoked her cigarette and sorted out her clothes for the day. A staff uniform for the local supermarket hung behind the door. Four nights a week, Judith spent three hours stacking shelves. Another five mornings she acted as receptionist for a wood merchant's across town. It was a family business, and the daughter-in-law took over in the afternoon when her kids went to nursery school. Judith was dreading them starting full-time, knowing it would probably mean the end of her job. Piss poor though the pay was, it was something. Family credit topped up a lousy wage and made sure she got help with paying rent on the two-bedroomed flat, so they managed. Just. Though she dreaded every new expense that came along.

She fished a dark skirt out of the wardrobe and went to fetch the iron, pausing by the bedroom door. Unhooking the uniform from the back of the door revealed a cheap, distorted mirror.

'My God, just look at yourself,' Judith muttered, leaning forward to examine the dark shadows beneath her eyes.

8.30 a.m.

Stacey was dressed and ready to leave. She sat beside the hospital bed in a high-backed chair. Her long blonde hair was drawn back from a pale bruised face, and the marks from the attack showed clearly on her throat.

Mike sat down on the bed. 'Hello, Stacey,' he said. 'I'm Detective Inspector Mike Croft. I was here last night.'

She looked at him and managed a weak half-smile. 'I don't really remember,' she said. Then, 'They say I can go soon. I'd like to go home if that's all right?'

He saw her swallow nervously and nodded. 'Of course. I'll keep this short. Is someone going to pick you up?'

'My mum and dad. They'll be here soon. Look, I told everyone everything I could last night, do I have to go through it all again?'

Mike shook his head. 'If you want me to go away and leave you alone, I will,' he said. 'If you want someone with you while you talk, then that's fine too.'

She stared at him for a moment, then took a deep breath and nodded her head. 'I'll be all right,' she told him. 'I'm sorry, it all happened so fast. I never thought I'd fight like that, but I just knew that I was going to die and every time I close my eyes I'm there again, with his

hands round my throat and his breath on my face and . . .
They gave me something to make me sleep last night and
it was worse than if they hadn't. He kept chasing through
my dreams, his hands all over me and I couldn't wake
up enough to get away.'

'I'm sorry,' Mike said softly.

They both fell silent for a moment, Stacey biting her
lip and staring at the floor. A nurse hovered discreetly in
the background, folding the sheet corners of another bed
and smoothing the covers.

Mike began again. 'Is there anything more you can
remember, Stacey? Something really small maybe that
came back to you?'

Still staring at the floor, she shook her head. 'No,
nothing. I told them all I knew last night.'

Mike decided that he would get no further. He could
see her parents walking down the ward, anxious looks
creasing their faces.

'You've been given the numbers to call if you need
anything or if there's anything you want to add?'

She nodded again. 'You're the one investigating?' she
asked. 'It is you?'

'My boss, Superintendent Flint, he's the one in
charge,' Mike told her. 'But . . .' he smiled.

'You'll be the one doing the work,' she finished for
him, trying to smile properly this time.

Stacey's parents had reached the bed. Mike introduced himself again, but they remembered him from the
night before.

'We can take her home now?' Stacey's mother asked.
'She'll be better off there.'

'Of course.' Then a thought struck him. 'Stacey, the man who attacked you. How did he smell? I mean, was he wearing aftershave, anything like that?'

She looked puzzled, frowned, really trying to think.

'No,' she said. 'No, I'm certain of it. He smelt kind of clean, if you know what I'm saying. Not over-scented or anything, just kind of soapy and clean.'

Price had waited for him in the corridor. When Mike got to him he was leaning against the wall, gazing out of the opposite window, a plastic cup of coffee in his hand and an expression of complete boredom on his face. He was trying to ignore the sound of Christmas carols drifting out of the children's ward.

He brightened when he saw Mike. 'She remember anything more, guv?'

Mike shook his head. 'She looks like the others, small and blonde.'

'She's the first one you've met, isn't she?'

'Yes, but I've had a good look at the pictures.'

They left the hospital and walked across to where they had parked the car. 'So, what do we have?'

'Six victims,' Price said. 'Age range fourteen to twenty-two, though the youngest was all made up to go on the pull and could have looked older and the eldest could easily have passed for seventeen. This one had her eighteenth birthday just last month. Make of that what you like.' He frowned. 'We've got an eighteen-month span timewise.'

'As far as we know.'

'As far as we know, and the attacks have been more violent as time's gone on. The fourth and fifth girls could have died.'

'So could this last,' Mike observed.

'True. But it seems to me he only got really vicious when she tried to fight him off. She hurt him, he retaliated.' He paused. 'Look at it the other way, mind, girl number four, Tracy Wilding, she didn't fight. She stayed passive, tried to keep him calm and got her head caved in for her trouble.'

They reached the car. Price slid into the driver's side and started the engine.

'No sign of him using a weapon this time,' Mike observed. The two previous victims had been hit with something hard and blunt-edged.

'Just his hands. No, but it's not the first time we've seen that. Tracy Wilding had choke marks round her neck, if you remember?'

Mike nodded. 'Then we've got two of the victims mentioning some kind of scent or aftershave. This one described him as clean and soapy.' He paused, picturing in his mind the street map pinned to his office wall and the six pins marking the places where the attacks had taken place. 'All open, public places,' he continued. 'Four parks, one common and one multi-storey car park. We know each time the attacker went some distance on foot, but there's nothing to say there wasn't a car parked close by, or that he hopped on a bus.'

'Not after attacking Tracy Wilding and Debbie Hall, he didn't. There'd have been too much blood.'

'OK, so it's likely he used a car. So he's fully mobile.'

He waited thoughtfully before continuing. 'So, what does he do? Cruise around looking for small blue-eyed blondes or does he pick his victims first and wait for an opportunity?'

'Not very likely, guv. Way I see it, he gets the urge and goes hunting.'

'How many hunts before a strike? And if he doesn't find what he's looking for, what then?'

Price glanced at him. 'You reckon the more violent attacks came after a few failures?'

'I think it's possible, yes. And then, then we have the letters. IF they're genuine.'

'If they are, it could be the one thing we really have going for us. This need to show off, laugh in our faces.'

'He hasn't fallen over his ego so far,' Mike commented.

Chapter Seven

DCI Charlie Morrow rubbed his hands together. 'Right, boys and girls, and what do we have on our fire this bright morning?'

'We totalled twenty-seven calls following the radio news this morning. Mostly missing persons. Two from drivers on the Devizes road last night, saw someone trying to hitch a lift.'

'Heading which way?'

'Back towards Malmesbury. About three or four miles from Kennet.'

'Description? Or is that too much to hope for?'

Sergeant Cooper shrugged. 'Male,' she said, 'average height, slim build.' She grinned. 'Apparently looked very wet.'

Morrow grunted what might have been a laugh. 'Well, he bloody would be, wouldn't he? What we have to hope is he looked wet enough for someone to take pity on him and pick him up.'

'We've got the same name coming in twice on the missing persons.' DC Stein had spoken this time. Morrow turned to fix the probationer with his usual malevolent stare. 'And?'

'Well, sir . . .' The younger man was starting to blush, Morrow noted. 'Well, sir, it seems a bit odd, sir.'

'Well, sir, it seems a bit odd, sir,' Morrow mimicked

viciously. 'Well, constable, maybe you'd like to do follow-up on that one.' He turned back to Sergeant Cooper who was eyeing him with open disapproval. 'Any "Mispas" we don't already have on our list, Beth?'

She nodded. 'Twelve, all from outside our area. Five of those known or thought to have been headed in this general direction. Usual mix, couple of New Age sorts travelling together. Teenager who had a holiday down here last year. Ran away from home and her parents are trying every direction. One mental patient, known to be suicidal. That one looks promising actually, sir; same age range, height and blood group as our victim. The fifth is a woman reported missing by her husband. Says she disappeared after a row and he knows she had relatives someplace hereabouts.' She paused. 'But he doesn't know where or what their names are.'

'Well, get on to his local plod station and tell them to go dig up his garden! Next?'

'The other Mispas are the usual "hoped-fors" I'd guess,' Beth Cooper continued unperturbed.

'Hoped-fors?' This from Stein, who was obviously trying hard to stand the Charlie Morrow test.

'Hoped-for result,' Morrow told him abruptly. 'Hell of a lot of folk out there would rather know for certain someone's dead and gone than spend the rest of their lives waiting for them to walk back through the front door.'

'But surely, sir . . .' Stein began and coloured red again.

'But surely, nothing,' Morrow told him. 'Now stop blushing like a frigging virgin and get some checking done. Start with that twice-reported Mispa.' He glanced across at Beth Cooper once again. 'I take it she's one we've already got on our list.'

Beth nodded. 'Yeah, name of Marion O'Donnel. Funny thing though, the new report comes from a name we didn't have as a contact before. I checked.'

'Interesting,' Morrow said. 'Well, you'd better go along with Stein. Hold his hand for him while he talks to these newly concerned friends.'

'Sir.'

'Any questions?' He glanced around the room at the dozen or so people he had allocated to him. He looked from the assembled officers to the stack of paperwork on his desk, the lines of enquiry that needed following. Callers that needed talking to, names to be checked and dead ends to be weeded out. Not enough bloody resources, he thought grimly, as bloody usual.

'OK, back at sixteen hundred hours. Bear in mind if you please that the Chief Super's yelling for results and after my backside.' He paused, fixing Stein with his discomforting gaze once more. 'That's supposed to be incentive to succeed, blushing boy, not to let things slide.'

There was brief laughter and Stein coloured again. Beth Cooper awarded Morrow a look that would have burned ice before guiding the embarrassed probationer towards the door.

It was cruel, Morrow knew, but some people were just made to be wound up.

He watched them go, then crossed to the white board on which was pinned the photographic record of the case so far, staring hard at each of the stark and brutal images.

'Who are you?' Charlie Morrow asked the dead woman. 'And who hated you so much that you had to die that way?'

Stein looked uncomfortable out of uniform. He was one of those people, Beth found herself thinking, who was happiest when he had an appearance of authority to hide behind.

Their destination was a neat terrace in Devizes itself, not far from the brewery. Beth got out of the car and glanced up at the house. Weak sunlight was trying to battle through thick grey cloud. Light caught the edge of the open transom window in an upstairs room.

'Well, looks as though someone's in,' she said. 'Hopefully, they're up and dressed.'

They were. Moments later she and Stein were introducing themselves to two neat, grey-haired women – 'The Misses Thompson' – who examined their IDs before ushering them both inside.

'So she was a regular visitor?' Beth checked as she took her cup of tea from the low coffee table that occupied most of the centre of the room.

She was conscious that they had been shown, as potentially important visitors, into the front parlour. Tidy with disuse and slightly chill, until the fire had been on for several minutes.

'Regular? Yes, I suppose so, since she moved back this way. We'd always kept in touch, you see. One of my best students. It took a lot of persuasion to get her father to agree to university. I know it seems funny in this day and age, but he was an old-fashioned man and couldn't see the point of girls having that sort of education. Always argued that all they did was get married and have babies whatever you taught them, so why waste time?'

'But he agreed in the end.'

'Oh yes, and he was there – we both were – the day she graduated. Dear Lord, I thought the man would burst, he was that proud.' She shook her head, laughing. 'People can say what they like on a general level, you know, but when it's their own – oh well, that's very different.'

'She was Dolly's final year,' her sister put in. 'Dolly went back, you see, after she'd officially retired. Taught part-time for another seven years.'

Edith, the younger sister, sounded more than a little in awe.

'Oh, do give over, Edie dear,' her sister told her. 'I enjoyed every blessed minute of it. But yes, Marion was one of my last students.'

'Is this her, Miss Thompson?' DC Stein was asking. He'd got up and was examining a graduation picture of a pretty, curly-haired girl dressed in gown and mortarboard.

Dolly Thompson nodded. 'Yes, that's Marion.' She sipped at her tea and then looked hard at the young woman opposite. 'You think it might be her, don't you?'

'Oh, Dolly,' her sister began. She fell silent as Dolly raised a hand to silence her.

'You think it might have been her in that car.'

Beth Cooper set her cup carefully on the edge of the

table before replying. 'Why did you call this morning?' she asked. 'Had something happened to make you suspect it might have been Marion in that car?'

The older woman continued to regard her in silence for a moment longer, then she said, 'I suppose you'd call it instinct. Intuition, perhaps. I knew, we both knew. Oh yes we did, Edie,' – this as the sister began to protest – 'that there was something not quite right the last time Marion came. She seemed distracted, anxious, and when she left her bag behind I began to wonder.'

'She left some things behind?'

'People do that all the time,' DC Stein put in.

'Yes, but generally they go back for them, especially when the things are so obviously personal.'

'What was in the bag, Miss Thompson?' Beth asked her.

'Just a few things. Letters, a cardigan, some keys I think and a poem. It was rather pleasing as I remember. Don't worry, dear, you won't have to ask. I'll give you her things before you leave. And her address too and that of her aunt. Her father passed on some two years ago now. Not an old man. It was very sad. But she has an aunt still living, sister of her mother's. And a small flat of her own in Malmesbury, if the landlord hasn't assumed she's done a moonlight and let it again.'

'Miss Thompson,' Aiden Stein was asking, 'why did you take so long before you reported her missing?'

'We didn't, dear, not really. You see, as I was about to tell you, Marion called on us about once a month. Usually the second Thursday, her day off, you see. When she left the bag behind I called her. She'd come and fetch it, she said. But there was nothing that couldn't wait and they had a rush on at work. Oh dear. I forget what it was.'

'Stocktaking or something,' Edie said helpfully.

'Yes, yes, well, whatever. So it wasn't until she didn't arrive on her usual day. And she hadn't called us to change her plans. We kept the day clear for her, you see, so she always called if she couldn't come.'

'Marion was like that,' Edie said. 'Always thoughtful.'

'So we left a message on her machine. In fact we left several messages. And called her aunt as well, but she seemed to think that Marion had gone away for a few days. Something about a new man in her life. When Marion didn't get in touch and she couldn't reach her, she did finally talk to the police. But your people just told her Marion was an adult, there was nothing they could do.'

She hesitated as though uncomfortable about something. It was Edie who said, 'She wasn't that good a judge of men, you see. Always did pick the unreliable ones. Her aunt was worried. We were worried. It was the way she didn't like talking about the man that concerned us.'

Dolly glanced gratefully at her sister. 'It made sense then, her not getting in touch. If she'd got herself involved and was worried we might not altogether approve. If this man wasn't quite right in some way. So . . .' She shook her head sadly. 'So, we did nothing and then I heard the news this morning and I just felt . . . there was no reason, dear, not really. Just an old woman's intuition I suppose.'

'How long since you last saw Marion?' Beth asked gently.

'I looked at the calendar, dear. It was two weeks. Exactly two weeks.'

'And when did you last speak to her before that, Miss Thompson? You said you called.'

'Yes, yes. It took a few attempts to get her. She didn't always leave her machine switched on and she was often out, so it was the Monday after her last visit. Ten days ago . . .'

'And how did she seem?' DC Stein asked.

'A little strange,' Dolly Thompson said. 'I thought about it a lot. I wondered if she just seemed strange in retrospect. You know, as if I'm adding that to the way she was because that's what I'm expecting her to be. But no. She *was* a little odd. A touch distant and impatient to get off the phone. She said she was expecting a call.'

'Maybe she was. From the new boyfriend perhaps,' Aiden Stein suggested.

'Maybe so. Maybe so.'

Dolly got up and went into the other room, returning with a macramé shoulder-bag lined with a bright blue print.

'This was hers,' she said. 'I glanced through, I was worried there might be something she might need inside. But it's all just as she left it. And you should have this.' She handed them another photograph of Marion O'Donnel. Written on the back were two addresses, her flat and her aunt's house. Along with her date of birth. Beth noted that she was twenty-five.

It was obvious that the interview was at an end. That

Dolly Thompson wanted now to be left alone with her sister. Beth took the bag from her and smiled encouragingly at the women. For the first time since their arrival Dolly Thompson looked her age, as though the handing over of the bag had forced the last piece of the puzzle into place. Made it certain that their Marion was dead and gone from their lives for ever.

DC Stein drove and Beth Cooper radioed in to Charlie Morrow. The DCI told her to look in the bag, give him a résumé of its contents and then report back to the station.

'It's a bit of an odd collection, guv,' Beth told him. 'A white cardigan, cable knit, a couple of paid utility bills, both for her flat by the looks of it.' She glanced more closely. 'Must have paid them at the post office in Devizes from the look of the date stamp. Then there's a letter.' She slid it carefully from the envelope, touching as little as possible. 'Signed Auntie Nora. That must be the other address we've got. Sounds like she's Marion O'Donnel's only relative.'

'Well, you'd better talk to her next,' Morrow instructed. 'Anything else?'

'Mmm, bunch of three, four, five keys,' she said, leaving them where they lay in the bottom of the bag. 'And another letter. No sorry, guv, it's not a letter, it's that poem Miss Thompson mentioned.'

'A poem. Right. Hand-written?'

'No. Typewriter, or printer. I'd say more likely printer,

there's no indentations on the paper and it's pretty thin stuff.'

There was silence over the radio as Charlie Morrow processed the information.

Beth waited.

'Go and talk to the aunt. Show her the stuff, she might have some idea. Maybe her niece wrote poetry. What's it about anyway?' he added impatiently.

'Well, that really is the interesting part,' Beth told him. 'It seems to be about West Kennet and a fire being lit up on the hill.'

Chapter Eight

They had not printed his letter. The morning paper carried an update on the latest attack, the revelation that the young woman had fought back and might have marked her attacker's face, but there was no mention of his letter.

The woman sitting across the breakfast table poured more tea and pushed the cup in his direction. He murmured thanks and continued to scan through the inside pages.

It wasn't there, no mention anywhere.

Perhaps it had simply been too late for the morning edition; he'd pushed the letter through the door the night before, and it had been late. Too late maybe for it to be printed in the morning.

He reached out and picked up his cup, sipping tea and allowing the loose page of the paper to rest against the teapot.

His face was sore where the girl had clawed at it with her key. Little bitch! There were bound to be stupid jibes from his workmates when they read the paper. Bitch! he thought again. His sudden surge of anger making his hand shake, he splashed his tea on to the blue-checked cloth.

Jane Adams

9.45 a.m.

The morning was chill and damp, the overnight rain soaking the fallen leaves and making the paths greasy underfoot.

Mike and Sergeant Price arrived at Aston Park at nine forty-five, slipping through the cordon, watching the search that had already been under way since first light.

The sergeant in charge crossed over to them.

'Anything?'

'Not a sausage. The rain's washed out any prints. We've got crushed grass and broken branches where the struggle took place but bugger all else.'

Mike nodded, he'd expected nothing more. In this instance the best hope for forensics was the victim herself.

He watched a little longer, the slow, thorough process of finding and bagging fragments of rubbish, examining ground too wet to hold a decent print, then he turned to go.

'The *Chronicle* offices next,' he said. 'See what Tom Andrews is excited about, then we'll go and find out if they've resurrected my car.'

Price rolled his eyes. 'Local garage got Jesus working for them have they, guv?'

Tom Andrews, senior staff reporter on the *Chronicle*, passed the letter in its plastic bag across to Mike and sat back waiting for the questions to begin.

'When . . .?'

'It was there this morning, hand-delivered, near as we can guess between eleven last night and three this morning.'

'Oh?'

'Last shift cleared out just after eleven. Sid the security man picked it up and put it on the front desk at about three, so . . .'

'So maybe our man works shifts?'

'Or was coming home from the pub, or out walking the dog.'

Mike nodded and read the letter again. The typeface was clear and uniform. Daisy-wheel maybe but more likely something like a bubble-jet printer. At least, that's what documents had said about the other two. Plain white sheet of typing paper and a cheap manila envelope, easily picked up at any stationer's or post office and a lot of other places besides.

And if it was like the other two there would be no prints – except, presumably, for Sid the security man's. With that in mind he said, 'I take it this Sid of yours has gone off duty?'

Tom Andrews nodded. 'He'd gone and his day relief was on by the time this was passed to me. You want to talk to him?'

'Get him to call in to divisional. Have his prints taken for elimination, that should be it. He can give a brief statement as well, just to keep the record straight as regard to time, but there's not much else.' He paused. 'You've taken a copy of this?'

'It's news, Mike. Look, we held off printing the other two because Flint strung us the line that the case was about to break. Didn't want the investigation jeopardized. So OK, we went along with him even though I knew he was lying through his teeth, but I mean, Mike, you can't expect the editor to hold off for ever. This is news, and there's bugger all else happening with this business yet.'

He regarded Mike thoughtfully. 'You've got an angle on this, I'll play it for all it's worth, but it goes in the next edition whether, which or how.'

'And the other two letters?'

Andrews nodded. 'Along with our reasons for sitting on them this far.' He smiled suddenly, the deep wrinkles creasing around tired grey eyes. 'Anything new come out of this latest attack?'

Mike leaned back in the chair and stretched his long legs. 'Plenty. Too much maybe. It's being weighed and sifted as they say.'

Tom Andrews gave him a shrewd look. 'Something on your mind?' he said encouragingly, then laughed as Mike shook his head.

'You know better than that, Tom.'

'I can always hope. Even DI Croft has his weak moments. If you want me to play an angle on this you'll have to let me know fast. I've got an editorial meeting in fifty minutes.'

Mike got to his feet. 'I'll give you a call.'

Tom Andrews watched him go, his eyes narrowing slightly as the tall man went through the swing doors and strode out into the car park. He had known Mike Croft some two years now, had come to like and respect him in that time, and had learnt to recognize when there was something preying on the man's mind. Something new and something very big.

As Mike got into the car, Price asked, 'He's going to publish?'

Mike nodded, took the plastic-wrapped letter and envelope from his pocket and handed it to the sergeant.

'And he's right,' he said. 'Nothing I can say that's reason enough to stop him.'

'Flint will not be pleased.'

'Superintendent Flint is never pleased. You're right though, but that's the least of our worries.'

Price handed the letter back to him and started the engine. This letter, which like the other two taunted the police for their lack of progress and threatened further incidents, was only a small part of what worried Mike. Tom Andrews had been right. Mike did have much more on his mind. There had been blood on Stacey's keys and on her clothing that had definitely not been her own. Blood was something they hadn't had before, but they'd typed the attacker from serology tests done on semen left at two of the previous crimes. The serology had shown the attacker to be type O.

The blood, of which there was sufficient quantity to leave no doubt, had been type A.

It had been a shock to Mike to realize that he had been dealing with two rapists and not just one. He was not yet ready to let Tom Andrews in on that fact.

Jane Adams

1.45 p.m.

Max Harriman took a slight detour on his way to work. He liked the two till ten shift best of all. It gave him his mornings free and didn't end so late that he was unable to indulge in other activities in the evening.

His detour took him through Aston Park, within a few yards of where the girl had been attacked last night. A police cordon had been thrown up around the area and Max could see the search team still probing the bushes for clues.

Max stood and watched them for a couple of minutes. He wasn't the only one; others paused too, fascinated by this glimpse into another, official world. Then he walked on slowly, his gaze drifting from the three men poking around in the bushes to the other two standing a little apart, looking at a map.

Max wondered what they'd found so far. He looked around, making certain that no one could see, then he lifted his hands close to his face, first fingers and thumbs at right angles as though framing an image. Smiling to himself, Max panned his imaginary camera across the scene.

Chapter Nine

Terry sat in the big chair in the corner of Maria's consulting-room. He was restless, moving constantly as though the chair was uncomfortable and he couldn't work out how to sit. His dark hair flopped forward over one eye as he stared down at his feet, turning them this way and that as though examining the laces.

Maria, sitting over by the window, the angle of her chair set obliquely to his, ignored the fidgeting. She had grown used to it; this sense of pent-up energy Terry exuded was symptomatic of a boy impatient to get away in time for football practice and had little to do with any clinical problem he might have.

Personally, she hardly viewed these sessions as therapeutic, or as making the best use of her psychiatric skills. The boy was in no need of medication, little need of deep therapy. Any trained counsellor could do what she was doing with him. He talked freely about his experiences and his feelings, trusting her, now, in a way that was very satisfying. In view of what he had been through, his mental balance was extraordinarily good. So good in fact that Maria was forced to wonder occasionally if she was missing something. If under the very moderate, very ordered façade lurked a clever manipulator. A psychopathic personality conning the expert.

Mostly, she preferred to believe that he was a very

ordinary teenage boy, emerging from a bloody awful past with far more determination and courage than could reasonably be expected. She held out great hope for Terry.

He had finally told her about Sarah and about 'some old woman' he had befriended who lived up the road from him.

'Her shopping bag broke,' he told Maria. 'I gave her a hand with her stuff and we kind of got talking.'

He stopped fidgeting for long enough to look up and meet her eyes, a Terry sign that this was important.

'She's all right,' he said. 'Used to be an actress, she's got books and books of cuttings, you know, all her reviews and stuff. We got talking about it. She even played on Broadway once.'

Maria nodded. 'And you've been to her house?'

Terry looked uncomfortable. 'Yes, like I told you. She showed me her scrap-books and stuff.' He fidgeted again but tried to hold Maria's gaze, something she knew he found terribly hard. 'Look, I know I should have told you about her and about Sarah, but I mean, do I have to tell you everything?'

'No, of course not.' She smiled. 'I know, sometimes it's hard to explain, the way a complete stranger can become a friend almost overnight.'

He regarded her suspiciously for a moment, seeing if she was testing him, winding him up.

Then he nodded. 'Yeah, it's kinda hard. But I like her. And there's Sarah too.' He frowned suddenly. 'Do they have to know, I mean about . . .?'

'That's not for me to say, Terry,' Maria told him. 'But

you should have a chat to your social worker about them both, especially Sarah, if things get serious.'

Terry frowned again. 'Nobody "chats" to Mrs Williams,' he said irritably. 'I suppose if I don't say anything, you'll have to tell.'

'No,' Maria shook her head. 'What you tell me is confidential, you know that.'

Terry stared at the floor, his shoulders tense. Maria knew how important these fledgling relationships were to him. Knew he was waiting for her to comfort. To encourage. Instead, she remained silent and waited for him to speak.

'I will,' he said at last. 'I will talk to her, but not yet. 'It's too soon. I don't want to ruin everything.' He gave her an odd sideways look as though challenging her to go against his wishes. The expression in his eyes caused Maria a moment of real doubt. It was so hard and so very cold.

7.55 p.m.

Sarah had been doing homework at a friend's house after school. Her mother collected her in the car rather than let her catch the bus home alone with all the worry of the recent attacks.

'I don't mind too much if there's two of you together,' Paula, her mum, had said in familiar refrain, 'but you're not coming home alone.'

Friday night was her mum's aerobics night and Paula collected her on the way to the class. It meant an hour of watching sweaty women in multi-coloured multi-stretchy sports gear leaping around to the strains of a badly set-up tape player, but Sarah had her magazine and figured she could cope.

The aerobics class was held in the gym of Fairfield Community College. They arrived just before eight fifteen, the evening wet and already cold, the car park yellow with the glow of sodium, discolouring the soaking tarmac.

'Oh, look after this, will you?' her mother asked her, dragging the mobile phone and her Visa card out of the glove compartment. 'And don't let me forget, I've got to get some petrol on the way home.'

'OK.' Sarah took the card and posted it absently into the pocket of her jeans. Her mother plucked her sports bag off the back seat, almost spilling her towel and after-class clothes on to the floor of the car as she stuffed the mobile phone inside. 'Hurry up now,' she said, shivering in her Lycra with just a sweatshirt pulled down over the top. 'I'm freezing.'

They crossed the car park and pressed the buzzer next to the glass doors, waiting for the light to flash in the gym so someone would come and let them in.

Moments later, a woman in pink Lycra and silver trainers came running down the hallway, pressed the button to release the catch and greeted Paula effusively.

'Are you joining us tonight?' This to Sarah.

'Oh no, our Sarah's not into aerobics,' her mother said. The two women laughed as though at some big joke and Sarah's mother smiled at her, a private smile, as though to apologize that they found it funny. Sarah smiled back, falling behind the two of them, following them to the gym with her magazine rolled tightly in her hand. She glanced at her watch. Ten minutes before the class began and then another hour. She wondered, not for the first time, why perfectly sane women – and, generally, she actually liked her mother – behaved like idiots when they got together.

She seated herself at the end of one of the benches in the gymnasium and settled down with the problem page of her magazine. Half an eye watching as the women took off their sweatshirts and coats, talking noisily, comparing, she thought with more amusement than cruelty, the sag of their respective tits and bums.

'OK,' the instructor called out, clapping her hands then bending to turn on the tape. 'Ready for the warm-up. One and two and side and stretch . . . get those knees higher girls . . . Remember, this is the last workout before Christmas.'

Sarah watched with half-attention.

Then the blue light began to flash.

'Reach higher, girls, higher . . . Oh, get that for me will you, love? Probably Debbie, she's always late.'

Sarah glanced across at the flashing light. She shrugged. 'Sure,' she said. She put her magazine aside and went to open the door.

8 p.m.

John Tynan turned into Cavendish Road. He had been looking forward to this evening. Theo was always good company and the young man, David, who had been lodging with her for the past eight months or so had proved to be very pleasant too in his own way.

He had been thinking earlier in the day about just how long he had known Theo. Most of her life, probably. Her older sister, May, had been at school with John's wife and the two had stayed friends all their lives, the two women dying within months of each other as it turned out, and from different versions of the same bloody illness.

May had lived all her life within five miles of where she was born, but Theo had always been a wild one. Wanted to be an actress and going full pelt to achieve her dream. She had run off to London and worked at anything and everything while she auditioned, until she'd finally got her first break with a little rep company that travelled doing one-night stands all over the country.

She'd done well for herself in the end though. In work more than out of it and playing small but useful roles on the television later in her career. Theo had stayed with sister May between engagements and kept in touch with old friends despite being away so much of the time.

It had been a great surprise when she'd come back home to stay. Must have been close on a year before, thought John.

He turned the corner into Cavendish Road to find his way blocked by a police car parked diagonally across the nearside lane and a uniformed officer waving the traffic around the cordon. Blue lights flashed eerily in the darkness pooled between the street-lights.

Theo's house. The cordon was around Theo's house. What the hell?

Anxious, John drove a little way on and parked at the side of the road, then walked back, taking in the two cars with their flashing lights. The constable standing by the slightly open door, the small crowd beginning to gather on the other side of the street and the curious watching discreetly from their curtained windows.

'You can't come in here, sir. I'm sorry, but there's been an incident.'

'But I'm expected,' John said, startled.

'If I could have your name, sir. And, you say you were expected?'

John took control of himself. 'My name is John Tynan, ex-Detective Inspector Tynan. Theo Howard is a friend of mine and I'd like to know what's going on.'

The young officer's expression had changed a little as he took this in. He opened his mouth to speak, but whatever he had in mind was interrupted as the front door was flung open and Davy threw himself out, grabbing at John's arm. His face contorted with emotion as he cried out, 'She's dead, John. Theo's dead!'

Tynan barely had time to react before Davy had been ushered gently but firmly into a waiting police car. He turned back, reaching a hand towards the closed door as though to push it open. It was white, he noted, as though seeing it for the first time. White replacement UPVC, with an ornate brass handle and a little stained-glass panel just above the letter box.

The young constable on duty was speaking to him, John realized, but it was not until the PC reached out and touched John's arm that he really took in what the man was saying.

'Are you all right, sir?'

'Yes, yes, I'm fine.'

'Was she a close friend? If you could just come and sit in the car for a moment . . .'

Another car had pulled up parallel with Theo's house. John saw it out of the corner of his eye and recognized Maria's silver Mazda. Mike was in the passenger seat.

John raced down the steps towards them, talking almost before Mike had a chance to get out of the car.

'Theo. They're telling me Theo's dead.'

'Steady, John, slow it down. What are you doing here anyway?'

'Theo, I told you, I came to see Theo.'

'She was a friend of your wife's,' Maria remembered as she eased herself out of the car. 'I remember you talking about her.' She frowned. 'Wasn't she an actress at one time?'

'Yes, yes. That's her. But they're telling me she's dead. I was supposed to come to dinner tonight. I got here to find the place cordoned.'

He took a deep breath as though realizing how close to hysterical he must sound, holding out a hand as though to fend off their concern. 'I'm all right, Mike. Really I am. It's just a bit of a shock.'

Another car arrived. The police surgeon got out, greeted Mike and nodded to John Tynan. 'Thought you were retired. Can't they keep you away?'

'Look,' Mike said, 'Maria will take you back home and stay with you.' He glanced across at her for agreement. 'Give me your keys, John, and I'll drive your car back later when I wind up here.'

For a moment Tynan's expression hardened as though angry at being dismissed. Then he nodded. 'But I want to know, Mike. I want to know what happened. Theo, she had no family, not since May died, same year as Grace you know. She was a good friend. A good friend.'

He allowed Maria to open the passenger door for him and got into the car, the age showing on his pale face as they drove away.

Inside, the house was tidy, no signs of a struggle. Unusually for a terraced house of this kind, there was a small hallway with the staircase going off. A little table, no larger than a plant stand, stood at the bottom of the stairs, supporting a red-shaded lamp.

Three doors led off the hall. One at the end, open to reveal the kitchen. The front room had been turned into a dining-room. Mike was directed into the rear living-room. It was not a large room. French doors led into a neat garden. A three-seater sofa, covered with a cream throw, stood against one wall with stacks of bright cushions propped against the ends. An old chesterfield with a drop-down arm stood at right angles to the first settee. It too was draped with cream, and blue cushions lay beneath the woman's feet.

Her shoes had been removed and placed tidily beside

the sofa. Other than that she was fully and smartly dressed in a dark green suit and cream silk blouse.

There was, Mike noted absently, a tiny ladder in the left foot of her tights.

Her head was supported on another blue cushion and her eyes were closed. Theo Howard had grey hair. It was shoulder-length and loose and there was something about the way it had been combed out across the cushion that made Mike look twice. One hand rested across her stomach, the other fell awkwardly towards the floor, but from her position, neatly propped upon the sofa, and the casual arrangement of her limbs, she could almost have been sleeping.

Almost.

The reek of vomit and alcohol filled the tiny room. An empty bottle lay upon the floor and streaks of vomit ran from her nose and the corner of the woman's open mouth, pooling beside her face, staining the blue of the cushion a fetid brown.

'She's holding something, Mike,' the police surgeon commented.

With gloved hands he gently opened the woman's hand. The fingers were still flexible, lightly clenched about the paper. Someone held an evidence bag for him and the surgeon eased the paper into the bag, drawing it flat as he posted it inside.

Mike took the sealed bag, moving away from the body as the surgeon continued with his work. Temperature of the body, temperature of the room, pronouncement of death at twenty thirty-two. Directing the photographer as she moved softly about the scene.

Mike read, his lips moving silently as he took in the words.

'Anything interesting?' the police surgeon asked.

'It's a poem,' Mike told him.

'A poem. Well, that's a new one.'

He packed his equipment away and prepared to leave. 'You can move the body when she's finished the family snapshots,' he said, nodding towards the photographer.

Mike thanked him. He glanced back at the paper in his hand and read again.

'Right now; I do not need to be told truth . . .'

Chapter Ten

8.40 p.m.

Charlie Morrow sat in the one and only armchair, trying not to think how long it had been since he last slept, and surveyed the rest of the room. It was a tiny flat. One small living-room, an equally small bedroom. Bathroom with a shower but no bath, crammed into a space that should have been a cupboard. A screened-off area at the end of the living-room that held a Baby Belling two-ring cooker, a sink and half draining-board together with a couple of wall cupboards and a yellow Formica-covered table that must have to double as a work surface.

Marion O'Donnel rented the place part-furnished apparently. The kitchen stuff was owned by the landlord, as was the bed – she'd supplied her own mattress. The two-seater sofa also came with the flat. It had a missing castor and its limp side was supported by folded cardboard torn from a cornflakes packet padded around a strip of wood.

The chair in which Charlie Morrow was seated, the pine desk standing under the window and the nest of square teak-effect tables were hers, it seemed. As were the assorted, cheaply framed posters and the flatpack bookshelves with their burden of paperbacks and magazines. Charlie Morrow had glanced through them earlier. She had eclectic tastes, he thought. A few thrillers, the odd romance. Cheap edition classics shoved, careless of any order, between science fiction novels, travel guides and women's magazines.

On the top shelf were framed photographs. Herself and two old ladies who must be the Misses Thompson. An old photograph of a man and woman, standing awkwardly together, the woman squinting into the sun with a hand raised to shade her eyes.

Another of the same man, older and alone, seated in the armchair that Morrow now occupied.

Others of Marion and younger people. College friends, he assumed. She looked relaxed and happy, laughing into the camera.

Charlie Morrow shook his head and sighed. 'Didn't know what was coming to you, did you, girl?' In his mind there was no doubt but that the dead woman was Marion O'Donnel. They'd contacted her dentist, got the dental records; it was only a matter of time until forensics confirmed what Charlie was certain he already knew.

Marion worked in a bookshop. They had tried to contact her when she hadn't turned up for work, but that was all. She had holiday due to her, had taken two weeks of it and then not come back to work.

'Was that in character?' Charlie Morrow had asked. Her employer had shaken his head. No, she had generally been reliable.

And you didn't think to report her missing? Morrow had questioned. The man had looked awkward. Shrugged vaguely.

'She was an employee, Detective Morrow. I don't think of myself as my brother's keeper, never mind my employees'. She was a nice girl, obliging and friendly with the customers. I'd had no complaints.'

'Until?' Morrow asked.

'Well, she'd . . . it was as if her mind wasn't on the job, suddenly. She came in late, pleaded sick and went early on, oh, a dozen or more occasions in the month before she took her holiday. And she started to forget things. Orders didn't get done and customers were complaining about her behaviour.'

'So you suggested she take some holiday?'

'I thought she might have problems. Need some time to sort them out . . . I don't know. She'd been a first-rate employee before, I didn't want to part with her if there was a chance she could straighten herself out. When she didn't come back, well, I thought . . .'

'That it was easier than having to get rid.' Charlie Morrow nodded, ignoring the man's indignation at his lack of tact.

'Was she close to anyone at work?'

Apparently not. She was friendly enough, but it was a small shop. Just himself, Marion and three part-timers. She had formed no close friendships with any of them.

Morrow took their names and addresses and arranged for interviews. By then it was getting late and he had come here to her flat, just as forensics were finishing up. Morrow looked at the stack of documents lying neatly on the desk.

She had been very ordered, he thought. Everything filed and kept. Bank statements arranged by date. Phone and other utility bills sorted according to type and held together with paperclips.

Personal letters in yet another folder.

There was nothing hidden between the pages of her books. Nothing slipped between the magazines. Her rent had been paid in advance and was up to date, or had been until two weeks before. The landlord, thinking she had been away, had let it slide for a week then dropped her a note through the door and, later, left messages on her answering machine.

'I thought there must be some good reason,' he had told Charlie Morrow. 'Eighteen, nineteen months she'd been with me. Paid her deposit good as gold and never so much as a day late. I decided she must have, maybe, family trouble and couldn't get back. So I said to my wife, I said, we'll take the rent out of her deposit money this month and she can make the deposit up again when she comes back.'

Charlie Morrow nodded and placed his own interpretation of events around the story, guessing it to be essentially the same but with a little of the altruism removed.

The landlord had been more worried about having police cars outside the converted house than he had been about the loss and possible death of one of his tenants.

There was a knock on the door; an officer came in and began to pack the sealed evidence bags into a plastic crate for transport.

Thoughtfully, Charlie Morrow reached out for the evidence bag lying on the table close to him. 'Here, you'll be wanting this too,' he said.

For him, that single sheet of paper was the most significant find of the day. A second poem, this one also untitled. It began: 'Right now; I do not need to be told truth . . .'

Charlie Morrow had been about to leave when DS Cooper and DC Stein arrived.

'Thought we might catch you, guv,' Beth said. 'We've just come from the aunt's place.'

'Anything useful?'

Beth shook her head. 'Not so far. The aunt was the father's sister; after Marion's dad died they didn't see a lot of her. No conflict or anything, just drifted apart.'

'Did the aunt know about the new boyfriend?'

Beth shrugged. 'She knew there was one, but that was about all. Thought his name might be Jack, but no last name and she'd never met him. Said Marion was a bit tight-lipped about this one. She reckoned that was unusual, Marion was generally full of it.'

'And the last time she saw Marion O'Donnel?'

'Was the Friday before Miss Thompson spoke to her on the phone.'

'And in her opinion, was her niece upset about anything?'

'Hard to say,' Beth shrugged. 'Marion stayed for maybe half an hour. Had a cup of tea, talked about work and family and then went on her way.'

'And did she mention the boyfriend then?'

Beth nodded, 'Briefly, only to say that she was still seeing him. The aunt seem to think he might be a married man. I think, because she was reluctant to talk . . .'

'And she said it wouldn't be the first time. Her last was a married man,' Stein put in.

Morrow nodded. 'That fits in,' he said, 'with what the Misses Thompson told us. That her choice of men left something to be desired.'

Chapter Eleven

8.40 p.m.

Sorting through the latest submissions to 'readers' wives' was not the most satisfying of deals. These, the static equivalent of mucky home videos – Jake got a fair few of those too, sent through his various agents – were always a mixed bag. Some of them, he thought, should have been wearing a bag. But on the other hand, he'd found some real hot sales that way.

She had been one of them. Vinnie had passed her photo on, he remembered. Vinnie had a good eye. She was a classic blonde, firm curves and that look. A little uncertain, a tiny bit shy, as though she didn't know the full score.

Whatever her boyfriend had been thinking when he took the shots, Jake saw pound signs.

And he'd groomed her, pampered her, dressed – and undressed her – right. Had her photographed by the best in the business. She could have had anything her little heart desired. But it hadn't been enough. She had to stick her pretty nose in where it wasn't wanted. Not satisfied with what she'd got.

For some people, he thought bitterly, nothing was ever enough.

Well, time to see how his latest project was doing. Jake set the photographs aside and went down into the basement.

When Jake first moved into the house the basement had been a damp and dismal place, crammed with the debris of generations of successive owners. He'd cleared it out, run power and heat and water into all three rooms and replastered the walls, hiding the cold stone behind a colour wash of broken white. The basement was virtually soundproof, warm, and each of the three rooms was decorated in its own distinctive style. Jake did a lot of his work from here and he needed comfort and variety, though he doubted the young man lying bound and blindfolded on the narrow bed had any appreciation of the effort he had gone to.

Jake had bound his victim's hands and feet and covered his eyes with thick grey ducting tape, but he had deliberately left the mouth uncovered. There was no need for silence. The man could scream himself hoarse and there'd be no one able to hear. And Jake had learnt the hard way how easy it was for someone to choke on their own vomit if you covered their mouths too tight.

He said nothing as he set the camera on its tripod, turning it towards the young man, checking he had the whole body in frame. The crotch of his jeans, Jake noticed, was wet, the damp patch spreading down one leg and on to the sheets.

'Who's there? For Christ's sake, who's there?' Voice cracked with desperation.

Jake said nothing. Panning down the body, then back to rest upon the face.

'Why don't you say something? I know you're there. For Christ's sake, why don't you say something?'

His voice broke and Jake could hear the young man

trying to control the sobs that rose in his throat. His face contorted with fear, his body writhing on the narrow bed as he struggled to turn his head, straining for the slightest sound.

Jake listened to him pleading, the voice thick with tears and the body twisting and convulsing with mental agony and the physical pain of arms tightly pinioned.

And Jake filmed it all, regretting only that he could not see the tears that would have stained the young man's face.

Chapter Twelve

Sergeant Price arrived at Fairfield just after nine. Sergeant Mason, his opposite number in the uniformed section, greeted him at the entrance. 'It's probably a waste of time you being here,' he said, 'but the mother's practically hysterical and two of the previous attacks took place not half a mile away.'

Price nodded. 'And the girl just went to the door and hasn't been seen since?'

'S'right. A blue light flashes in the gym when someone wants to come in. The door's released by this catch here. Gives you five seconds to get out before it closes again.' He shrugged. 'Not that it's much of a problem. The door lock can be blocked with chewing-gum – often is when the kids are in school and half the time in hot weather they prop it open with a litter bin. Unless the alarm's actually armed, and it won't be while the building's in use, there's nothing to tell anyone the door's been left unlatched.'

'Very security-conscious.' Price laughed without humour. 'But tonight it was properly closed?' He glanced up at the security camera above the door. 'Do we have the video tapes yet?'

'Someone from the security company's being sent over. Should be here within the hour. There's that camera there and another two trained on the car park.'

Jane Adams

Price looked towards where he pointed. 'Which anyone with half a brain cell could avoid by staying close to the walls.'

Mason nodded. 'Set up to deter car thieves, and petty vandals,' he said. 'I imagine they give a good view of the car park and the first-floor windows but not much else. And this porch affair makes that camera less than useless once you're underneath it.'

Price nodded. 'Well, we'll have to hope we get lucky. You'd better take me to the mother.'

Inside the gymnasium all was quiet. A small knot of women in training gear gathered around a woman sitting on a bench. A WPC, looking strangely out of place in her dark uniform, was taking statements. She saw Price and came over to him. The woman on the bench watched anxiously. Her hands clutched at the sweatshirt draped around her shoulders and her face looked pinched and tired.

'She's certain it's the sex attacker,' the WPC said. 'I keep telling her it's way off his MO, but the idea's got fixed in her head.'

'Any reason, I mean particularly?'

The WPC sighed. 'Because Sarah looks like the rest, sir. Fifteen years old, small and blonde and slightly built and because the mother's scared out of her wits. Wants any answer. Though it beats me, sir, if she's more afraid of her daughter being grabbed by some pervert or of going home to her old man and telling him about it.'

9.30 p.m.

Mike was getting nowhere.

'I know nothing, Inspector Croft,' David Martin was insisting, as he had been since the interview began. 'I came home around 7.30, the door was unlocked. I thought it was strange, but Theo's like that. It's one of those doors that you have to actually remember to lock. It doesn't latch on its own.' He looked at Mike as though for confirmation. 'Sometimes Theo just forgot.'

He paused, studied his hands clasped in front of him on the table. 'I called her name and I went through to the back room. She was just lying there. Just lying there the way . . . I thought she was sleeping. But she'd been sick . . . and then I saw the bottle.'

'And you tell us Theo had had a problem, but that she no longer drank at all.'

'She couldn't!' David Martin's voice rose again. 'I told you, Theo had a problem. A big problem, but she'd been sober more than a year. Completely dry for almost thirteen months.' He broke off and hammered with both fists on the table. 'And then your lot arrived and dragged me here. I should be with Theo, not sitting here with you going over the same bloody ground over and over again. I did nothing! I saw nothing! She was like that when I got there and I don't know what the fuck happened.'

Mike was silent and for a moment there was no sound in the room except for David Martin's laboured breathing. Agitated, David dragged his fingers through his hair and then rubbed both hands across his face, pulling at his skin as though trying to wipe reality away.

'She's really dead?' he asked, his voice cracking. 'Theo. She's really dead?'

'You were close friends?' Mike questioned.

'We were more than friends. Theo and I, we'd been lovers for, well, close to a year. She moved here and I followed on a couple of months later. I had some things to sort out first.'

'Things?'

'A . . . a job, that sort of stuff.' He lifted his gaze to meet Mike's and his voice rose angrily again. 'I had a living to earn. I wasn't going to sponge off her. And don't think I don't know what you're thinking. Younger man. Older woman. Just using her for what he can get.' He fell silent again, twisting his hands, his anger burning itself out once more.

'But no one knew of your relationship,' Mike reminded him. 'Why was that?'

The young man's eyes flashed. 'Because she was afraid. Scared of what everyone would say about us. Everyone like you, thinking the worst. Cheapening what we had.'

'Close friends would have understood,' Mike said quietly, thinking of John Tynan.

'Theo had no close friends. There was only me. The rest. The rest meant nothing to her.'

Mike let it pass. The young man's hands had grown still now and lay flat upon the table. He stared down at them, his gaze intense, but blank.

Mike let the silence sit for a little longer, Then: 'That scratch on the side of your face, Mr Martin. How did you get it?'

Saturday,
17 December

Chapter Thirteen

3 a.m.

Although it was now the early hours of the morning, the noise of the argument continued unabated. It had been interrupted, briefly, by Price's arrival, but soon resumed and as he went into the hallway to use the telephone he could hear the parents railing at each other even through two closed doors.

The noise became louder momentarily as the WPC who had been left to cope with the grieving parents slipped out after him.

'They been like that all the time?' Price asked her.

She nodded, wearily. 'More or less. I gave up trying to calm it down. I might as well not have been there for all the notice they were taking, so I thought that as long as they weren't actually coming to blows I'd let it burn itself out.'

Price gave her a wry smile. 'Grief takes people in different ways. That's what my old sergeant used to say when I was just a probationer.'

'Right sir; if scoring points off each other counts as grief, well, I'd say they're drowning in the stuff.'

Price grinned at her, his hand resting on the phone. 'Was there something you wanted to tell me or did you just need a breather?'

'Both! But yeah, there is something Mrs Myers told me about ten minutes before you got here. I'd have called it in, but I'd been told you were on your way and she seemed pretty keen on keeping it from her husband.'

'Oh?'

'The kid, seems there might be a chance she's taken it into her head to do a runner. I mean, if this was going on all the time . . .'

'She wouldn't get far, no money.'

'That's just it. She had her mother's Visa card.'

'She had what? She stole it?'

'No. Her mum didn't want the bother of taking her handbag, she'd just got her sports bag, so she asked Sarah to look after it for her. Sarah slipped it in the pocket of her jeans. She had it with her when she left.'

'Fucking hell! Why didn't she mention this hours ago?'

'Says she was too distressed and just forgot.'

'Forgot. All right, all right. I've got to call in about the video tapes. You go back to the battle of the bulge. I'll be there in a couple of minutes and we'll deal with this.'

She rolled her eyes. 'Thanks a lot, sir.'

Price, his hand still resting on the phone, nodded slowly, listening to the continued arguments. Silently, he hoped the kid bankrupted the pair of them.

Price was surprised to be put through to Mike Croft. 'What the hell you doing there, guv? Thought you were off tonight.'

'So did I. Suspicious death. What's your excuse?'

'Mispa. Christ almighty, we're never going to get the

overtime on this. I've clocked up thirty hours so far this month alone.'

Mike laughed briefly. 'So tell me another one. A Mispa, can't the new relief deal?'

'Well, it got a bit complicated.'

He explained briefly the details of Sarah Myers' disappearance. 'The mother's convinced it was the sex attacker. It's looking more and more as if the kid simply took off with her mum's credit card.'

'Anything useful on the video tapes?'

'Nah, not a lot. We've reviewed just the half hour either side of her going. It's the usual over-used tape and grainy pictures and it's dark and raining and the sodium lights create one hell of a glare. You know the problems. The girl left with someone, probably male, looks tall, but as Sarah Myers only stood about five two in heels anyone's going to look tall.'

'Probably male?'

'Well, it was wearing trousers, but so was Sarah. No, looked vaguely male but the hood of the coat was pulled well up so it's hard to tell anything more.'

'Anything to suggest she was being coerced?'

Price sighed. 'My instinct says no. But he had hold of her arm and at one point she pulls back, glances towards the door. So . . .'

'Right. Well, I'm just about to wrap up for the night. What's left of it. This one's going to turn out a little difficult, I think.'

'Why's that?'

'The dead woman, she was a friend of John Tynan's and he's going to be pushing for some answers.'

'Ah. Nasty. Is it definitely murder? Anyone in the frame yet?'

'I've got the lodger here making a statement but we don't even know what we're dealing with till I've got the PM report. The look of it is, she got drunk and choked on her own vomit, so . . .'

'Right. Well, I'm going to have to get going. I need to find out if this credit card's been used since the girl disappeared and if she has any relatives in the south of France she might have run off to.'

He signed off and replaced the telephone back in its cradle. Behind him the noise continued unabated. Price took a deep breath and went back to join the adult Myers.

3.40 a.m.

Maria had dozed off in the chair. She woke to find John bending over her, a mug of chocolate in his hand.

'I made us both one,' he said. 'But you ought to go to bed.'

'I'm all right. Sorry, John, I'm supposed to be keeping you company, not falling asleep on you.'

'I don't need a baby-sitter, my dear. I'm quite all right.' He paused, sitting down opposite Maria on the old sofa. 'I just wish he'd call.'

'I know, John. I know.'

Maria leaned back in the chair and sipped her chocolate. It was still too hot to drink properly. Her gaze travelled around the comfortable sitting-room that was so familiar now. The massive, carved wooden cupboard that took over one wall. The sagging, tapestry-covered furniture, chosen by John's wife years before and well past its retirement age and all the random collection of books and pictures and knick-knacks accumulated over long residence. Recently, a new photograph had joined the collection on the bookshelves. Herself and Mike, taken on a day at the seaside in July. She was in a summer dress, the skirt blowing in the usual east coast wind. Mike was in cream trousers and an open-necked shirt, head slightly bent to the side and that lost look he always had when someone took away his jacket and tie.

'He'll call, or be here, before long. I'm sure he will.'

John Tynan nodded, the lines gathering about his eyes as he tried to smile at her. 'It's just so hard, my dear. I want to be out there, doing. Not stuck here like some spare part unable to help, to influence a damn thing.'

3.45 a.m.

Money had been withdrawn from Mrs Myers' Visa account. Discovering that it had not been drawn until one fifteen that morning and that the transaction could have been blocked only added to Phillip Myers' anger.

'And it never occurred to you to mention it? Never thought it might be important, I suppose?' he shouted at his wife.

Why the hell does she put up with him? Price thought. He exchanged a glance with the WPC and said quietly, 'Did Sarah know your PIN number? Kids often see their parents drawing money. Do you think she would have known your number?'

Paula Myers nodded. 'Probably,' she said. 'I mean,' she took a deep breath, 'yes, of course she did. She'd been with me when I drew cash, I'm sure she would have seen.'

'And remembered?'

'My daughter is not a thief, Sergeant,' Phillip Myers said stiffly. 'Someone abducted her from the leisure centre and that same someone must have used the card.'

'You think they forced her to tell them the number?'

It was interesting, Price thought, that Myers found it so much easier to accept that his daughter had been kidnapped and forced to reveal the number of his wife's Visa card than it was to accept that she might have drawn the money herself.

'They wouldn't have had to force it out of her,' Myers said heavily, glaring at his wife.

'Oh, Phillip, please.'

'I'm not sure I understand, Mr Myers.'

Phillip Myers exhaled slowly. 'My wife,' he said heavily, 'as you cannot fail to have noticed, is not the brightest of people. Amongst other annoying little habits, she forgets her PIN numbers. I scratched her number on to the corner of her card so she wouldn't forget it yet again.'

'You did *what*?' Price could hardly believe it.

'And there was no damn need,' Paula Myers was saying. She had been seated at the dining-table, agitated fingers playing with the white lace cloth, but now she rose to her feet, her eyes blazing, more anger powering her slight body than Price had seen her display all night.

'I make one mistake with the card and you treat me like a complete fool. It's something anyone could get wrong, but no. It's just one more proof to you of your goddamned superiority. Well, let me tell you something, Phillip. That wasn't the only mistake I made. The biggest one, the first and most damning one, was marrying you and the second one was letting you have anything to do with raising Sarah. If she's run away it's because of you. Your fault.' She lay a shaking hand on her narrow chest, breathing hard. 'Not mine. *Yours*, because she hates you just as much as I do and what's more she's bright enough that no one had to teach her how to do it.'

Phillip Myers stared at his wife, momentarily silenced.

Price wanted to applaud; instead, he glanced appraisingly around the dining-room at the expensive and perfectly matched yew-wood suite and the display of fine china on the dresser shelves. Money, he thought. Money and stuff bought for show. Because they went well together, not because there would be any pleasure in their use.

Phillip Myers had recovered himself and was about to begin again. Price turned back to him with a question he'd been wanting to ask since he'd first arrived and seen lurid scratches on Myers' temple.

'Where were you on Thursday night, Mr Myers, between about six and nine?'

Jane Adams

4.10 a.m.

Mike arrived at Tynan's cottage just after four. The place looked to be in darkness and he breathed a sigh of relief, wanting rest rather than questions he couldn't answer right then. A tiny crack of light at the heavily curtained living-room window made him groan out loud. It had been too much to hope, really, that John and Maria would have gone to sleep, content to wait till morning for the news.

They must have heard the car because the door opened, flooding yellow light on to the step. The rain had stopped and the air smelt fresh and clean as Mike got out of John's car and walked wearily to the open door. He fancied he could almost smell the sea on the freshening wind. It was very cold and he was very tired.

'Not much I can tell you, John,' he said as he stepped into the narrow hallway, ducking his head instinctively under the crooked lintel above the door.

'How did she die?'

'We don't know yet, but it may well have been an accident.' He was aware that he had lowered his voice, dropped into that careful cipher he used for the distressed and the newly bereaved. Aware too, from John's face, that he had recognized the tone and resented it.

He apologized at once. 'I'm sorry, John. It's been a bloody night. Has for all of us.'

He shrugged off his coat and turned to kiss Maria who had emerged sleepily from the living-room. 'Mind if I make some tea? I've had three cups tonight, all of them cold and with that foul stuff in the plastic cartons instead of milk.'

John Tynan nodded, going into the kitchen to fill the kettle and setting it on the stove. Maria followed him, perching herself on the table edge, and Mike leaned against the doorframe, watching the gas flame lap around the kettle, willing it to boil quickly.

'You knew she had a drink problem?' he asked John.

'Yes, she told me when I took wine over to dinner. The first time I went to dinner with her. Before David went to live there.'

'Well, it looks as though she could have started over again. There was an empty bottle of scotch on the floor and she'd been sick. Until I get the PM report I can't say for sure, but . . . it happens. She was lying on the sofa as though she'd been taking a nap. If she was too drunk to wake up properly . . .'

John Tynan nodded. 'I see,' he said. 'And David?'

'He's made a statement. Until we know the time and cause of death there's nothing more to be done.'

The screech of the kettle's whistle tore into the quiet of the kitchen. John lifted it from the stove and switched off the gas. He turned away from them as he poured water into the large brown pot, stretched the absurd woollen cosy over the top and shook it gently as though that might speed up the process. Mike could see that for all his calm his hands were shaking and his lips were bloodless.

'She was one of the last, you see,' John said with quiet resignation. 'Mine was not a job that made for socializing. Well, you know all about that. Grace kept in touch with people but when she died, well, I wasn't much good at it. Theo was one of the last of our mutual friends.

People we'd both grown up with. It's a shock. She was so much . . . alive.'

He took a deep breath and straightened up, began arranging cups on the tray and sugar and milk. His hands shook a little and he was showing his age far more than usual.

'And what about David,' he asked. 'Where has he gone now? Presumably not back to the house?'

'No, we've got a cordon round the house until cause of death's certain. As I understand it he's gone to a hotel for the night. There's another thing, though. Our people arrived practically on his heels. Suspected break-in at the same address. Neighbours'd seen a teenage boy running away, climbing over that back wall and into the garden of the house behind.'

'Any connection with Theo's death?' Maria asked.

Mike shook his head. 'There's no evidence of a break-in. No disturbance that we could see. Of course, we can't be certain there was nothing missing.'

'You'll have David to check later on.'

Mike nodded, flexing his shoulders in an effort to clear some of the exhaustion from his body. He was very tired, but his mind was jumping and he knew he would be unlikely to sleep.

'Did you know they were lovers, John?'

'What, Theo and David?' He paused, poured the tea with a much steadier hand. 'I didn't know. Not for certain, but I did wonder. And if that's true, then I'm glad. I know that David made her very happy and if they were more than friends, well, all I can say is good for them.'

Chapter Fourteen

Jake held the cup to the young man's lips and told him to drink. His victim was whimpering now, pleading hysterically to be released, so frantic that he could hardly swallow. He choked on the water as Jake tipped the cup too fast, coughing and spluttering with the liquid pouring back out of his mouth and through his nose. Jake moved aside to protect his clothes, frowning slightly.

'Now, drink,' he repeated, tipping the cup again. The blond man managed to swallow this time, gulping convulsively. 'Don't want you dying on me quite yet,' Jake told him. 'Not quite yet.'

He moved out of camera shot, setting the cup down. The man was still blindfolded, but for the sake of the film, Jake had covered his own face. He wore a black ski mask and combat gear. A knife in his belt and an AK47 replica propped against the wall. This one would probably end up as just one brief sequence in the finished film, but Jake liked to participate from time to time, bit parts that extended his enjoyment of the make-believe. There was enough genuine footage around, available dirt cheap if you knew where to find it, for him not to be too worried about providing major scenes and he often doubted that his buyers would know the difference anyway.

He returned to the bed and checked the bindings

around the wrists and ankles. The tips of the fingers were cold and slightly blue, but not enough to cause immediate concern, and the ankles were puffy either side of the bindings. He took the knife from the sheath at his belt and laid it coldly against the blond man's throat.

'Can you feel this?' he asked.

No reply.

Jake pressed the point harder, just drawing blood. 'I said, can you feel this?'

'Yes, yes, I can feel it. I don't want to die. I just don't want to die . . .'

9.15 a.m.

The bell rang as he pushed the door of the small artist's supply shop and the girl looked up from the counter.

'Oh, hello, Mr Phillips, not your usual day, is it? I'll tell Freda you're here.'

Jake Bowen smiled at her. 'No, I don't usually make calls at the weekend, but I was passing and it's going to be a couple of weeks before I'm this way again.'

The girl nodded and went into the back of the shop to tell the owner that John Phillips had arrived. Jake put his briefcase down on the counter and began to sort out the supply catalogues Freda Hurst had requested. She was hoping to expand, was in the process of buying the shop next door and planned to add photographic and darkroom equipment to her stock. John Phillips, her usual rep, was all in favour.

Freda came through from the back of the shop, her face wreathed in smiles.

'Thanks for calling in,' she said. 'I hope it's not put you out?'

'Not at all, glad to help.' He placed the catalogues on the counter. 'Just give me a ring if you need advice.'

'OK, will do.' She was holding a newspaper in her hand and waved it at him. 'Dreadful business,' she said, pointing to the front page and the updated report of the attack in Aston Park.

Jake nodded sympathetically. 'It won't be long before they get him though, he's getting too cocky for himself if you ask me.'

Jake had seen the report earlier and he meant what he said. Back in his car he glanced at his own copy of the paper. So the prat was sending letters to the police now, was he? Jake shook his head. Amateur, he thought.

10.30 a.m.

Max Harriman had Saturday off. He lay in bed late, propped against the pillows, smoking a cigarette. He was as individual in this as he was in all things; cigarettes were an indulgence he allowed only before he took his morning shower. Max might like to smoke, but the stale smell of it on hair and clothes was something he found intolerable.

On the wall opposite the bed were pinned a series of images. They were nothing if not eclectic. There was a centrefold, the staple marks carefully smoothed away so as not to spoil the look of the woman's skin. Her name, according to the title at the top, was Marianne – though Max knew different . . .

Next to that was a picture cut from a full-page advert in a magazine. The blonde woman with the perfect smile and the blood-red lips gazing out at him. And positioned above them both, pictures taken with a motor wind of a teenage girl. Her blonde hair flying loose as she ran.

There were others too, of places Max had lived and people he had known. Obsessions he'd once had that had played themselves out on a much bigger screen than a mere still camera could embrace. An historic catalogue of Max Harriman's life and work.

The other one had taken those pictures for him, the ones of the young girl he'd liked so much and been torn away from before his time. Jake was good like that, he never said a word, just provided the images for Max's fantasies. Gave him the title and then watched him run with the story. Time to time, he'd even used the raw material Max could provide. Max was proud of that.

Max drew deeply on the cigarette. It was his third that morning, chain-smoked. He would allow himself one more. Then shower and dress and begin his day properly.

He was proud of his sense of discipline. It was important to be ordered, in most things at least; Jake had taught him that.

But even Jake broke loose sometimes from his strictly self-imposed rules. The first two girls here in Norwich, for instance, they had been his. The fourth one too, but the others had belonged to Max.

A tribute to the master one might say.

Max smiled, shook his last cigarette from the package and lit it from the butt of the last.

Chapter Fifteen

11 a.m.

Mike had been so certain that Theo's death was a tragic accident that he had not even called in to chase up the post-mortem.

He was well aware that, regardless of what TV dramas liked to portray, anything short of a dead cert killing had to wait in line with the other routine body count: the cot deaths, the sudden heart attacks, the collapses and the suicides and the unidentified. Theo's death would be lodged somewhere on this list and wait until someone could get around to dealing with it.

It was with deep surprise, therefore, that he took the call, standing in John's hallway in the middle of what he'd hoped would be a peaceful morning.

'I put her on the list for my students to take a look at,' the pathologist was saying. 'I like to give them a little variety and this was a good one. I'd got a couple of them doing preliminary exams and when they told me what they'd found I was certain they must be mistaken.'

'I thought you'd decided it was probably asphyxia?' Mike questioned, acutely aware of John's hovering presence in the background.

'That's right, but this is slightly off kilter. There's evidence of minute conjunctival haemorrhage. I've brought her to the top of my list, Mike, but from the early indicators, your lady was smothered.'

'The haemorrhage you found, it's not consistent with asphyxia caused by vomiting?'

'If there's vomit in the lungs then, yes, it's possible. Drowning on your own puke when you're blind drunk isn't that uncommon, as you well know, but it doesn't normally lead to the kind of pressure needed to rupture blood vessels in the eyes. It's more consistent with what we'd expect to find in strangulation or, as I think we've got here, smothering.'

Mike listened a while longer, thinking of the way Theo's body had been positioned. The bottle on the floor and the scattered cushions ... Blood alcohol had been found at 275mg per 100ml of blood. Enough to cause unconsciousness, Mike thought. Theo was very, very drunk. Killing her would have been easy.

He put the phone down and turned to face John. He didn't need to say a word.

'She was murdered, wasn't she?'

'We can't be certain yet.'

'You'll be bringing David in for questioning again?'

'When we get confirmation, yes.'

John nodded slowly. 'And the boy seen running away?'

'We've no news yet. I don't know, John, he could be completely unconnected.'

John Tynan took a deep breath and shook his head. 'I know you have a job to do but go easy on David.'

'I'll treat him the way I'd treat anyone else.'

'I know, I know. But I can't believe he's involved in this. I believe he loved her.'

Mike nodded. 'The number of killings committed by

strangers is pretty small, John. You're as much aware of that as I am. You didn't even know the pair of them were lovers until I told you. We still don't know that's true. Who can tell what their relationship was really like?'

'I saw them together. I knew Theo well.'

'But not David Martin. About him you know next to nothing. A few meetings when he showed you what he wanted you to see.'

'I'm not a fool!'

'No, no, you're not. But you are a friend.' He paused. 'Theo's dead, John. We don't know for certain that we're looking at murder, but if we are, I'm going to find out who and why, and there's no more that I can say.'

11.10 a.m.

Maria was catching up with the morning news when Mike came in to say he'd have to go. He explained quickly about the phone call.

'How's John taking it?'

'How do you think?'

Maria smiled. 'You're going to watch the PM?'

'Yes, I was wondering . . .'

Maria took the car keys out of her bag and handed them to him. 'We're going to book a day off, Mr Detective Inspector Croft, and we are going to take that junk heap of an estate car and see who's stupid enough to give you a trade in on it.'

She turned the local paper towards him. 'Have you

seen this? Oh, and there's a piece on Theo's death on page two.'

Mike took the paper from her. 'Yes,' he said. 'I've already read it.' He skimmed the front page again. Tom Andrews had played it very fair, he thought, though Superintendent Flint hadn't seen it that way. Mike had spoken to him on the phone earlier while Maria had still been catching up on sleep. 'Flint was not amused,' he said. 'Thinks all journalists should be operating under a D notice or kept to reporting on village fêtes.' He read out loud from the sections of the letters Tom Andrews had published.

> *There will be others.*
> *The police will never find me.*
> *I can run rings around them.*
> *I don't even have to try.*

'Your man believes in short sharp sentences,' Maria commented.

'Hmm, and that's not all, he lays them out like poetry, you know, double-spaced, each sentence on a new line . . .' Mike frowned, reminding himself of what Tom Andrews hadn't yet been told. As he now knew there were two attackers, which one was responsible for the sending of the letters, and why? The thought came fleetingly that the author of the letters might be deliberately taunting the other man. Hoping to goad him into further action. He turned back to Maria, bending to kiss her goodbye, enjoying the way she smelt, fresh from the bath. Marry me, he thought, but he didn't say it. Instead, he asked, 'And what does this say to your keen psychiatrist's brain then, Dr Lucas?'

'Well,' she said, taking back the paper, 'I should say, Inspector Croft, that what you have here is a bit of a nutter.'

2 p.m.

Charlie Morrow had long ago given up worrying about paid overtime, or weekends. The truth was, he didn't have a great deal else to fill his time. He had no family – a brief and broken marriage without children. Few friends outside the workplace – and there were those who would argue he had fewer in it. So, to find him working overtime on a Saturday was not so unusual.

Rain lashed at his office windows. December rain falling from a heavy sky. The office lights were on in an effort to offset the grey, but, somehow the yellow cast only made the room, with its threadbare green carpet and stained white walls, an even gloomier place.

Charlie Morrow sighed and put down the address book he had been studying. He'd worked his way through, so far, from A to E – including D for dentist – phoning through the list. Giving out a standard spiel. Introducing himself and his business and explaining who he was trying to trace. So far, the Thompson sisters were the last people who claimed contact with Marion O'Donnel. Idly, Charlie Morrow played with the scenario that the sisters might have done away with the young woman themselves. He could just picture the headlines:

'Thompson Twins in Inferno Murder', see himself arresting two twittering, grey-haired old ladies for a brutal killing.

Then he stopped laughing and got up, stretching. He was hungry and humour didn't work on an empty stomach.

He eased himself back into his jacket. It seemed to be going the way of all others and getting too small again. And, he thought, glaring out of the window, it was still bloody raining. Maybe that was the problem with his jacket, too often wet, it was obviously shrinking.

He packed the evidence bags away into his drawer and locked it. Dragged his green, waxed cotton raincoat off the hook and put it on, another button coming off between his fingers as he tried to fasten it.

Swearing to himself, Charlie Morrow dumped the button in his pocket along with the other junk, and went out to brave the rain.

3 p.m.

Maria had stayed with John Tynan until well after lunch, he had so obviously needed the company. Then she'd suggested that he come over to Oaklands the following day after work. They could go for a drink and a bite to eat in one of the local pubs. By the time she left, just after three, there had still been no further word from Mike and the waiting was trying John's patience.

It was pouring with rain again, and visibility on the narrow roads was further cut down by what promised to be an early dusk. Maria found herself thinking about Sarah, wondering if the girl was out in this and wanting to go home. Or if there was more to it than a teenage girl annoyed with her parents. That figure Mike had talked about on the video film still hadn't been identified. Maria really didn't want to think about the other possibilities. She was used to being on the front line of other people's distress, her job made sure of that, but it sometimes seemed to Maria that she'd seen more pain and human cruelty in the eighteen months since she'd met Mike than in all her working years.

6 p.m.

Outside, it was still raining. Charlie Morrow had reached T in Marion's address book. One thing he had learnt about Marion: she had an odd way of ordering her phone numbers. They weren't listed in any form or order that Charlie Morrow could figure out.

OK, he could understand D for dentist instead of the man's name, and GP for doctor was reasonable, but more often than not people seemed to be listed under their first name instead of their last, or according to some other reference he could only guess at.

He looked up the first entry under T and dialled the code and then the number. The phone was picked up on the third ring.

'Good evening,' he said. 'I wonder if you can help me. My name is Charles Morrow and I'm a detective inspector with the Devizes police. That's Devizes in

Wiltshire,' he added, realizing that he had no idea which part of the country he was calling. 'I'm trying to contact someone I believe may be at this number. Someone called Theo Howard.'

7.30 p.m.

By the time Mike arrived back at John Tynan's house he was very tired. The post-mortem on Theo's body had brought surprises and now, Mike realized, they were dealing with a whole new ball game. Driving through the twisting country roads back to the cottage, his mind played with the facts.

Fact number one, Theo Howard had been murdered. Fragments of blue fibre had been found in her mouth and nose and even the upper part of her lungs. The fibres matched the blue cushions on the sofa. The one on the floor next to the empty bottle had been stained with vomit.

Someone had killed Theo Howard by pressing the blue cushion over her nose and mouth and holding it there. Mike could imagine the final struggle for breath. Drawing only the soft, airless fabric into her nose and mouth.

Would she have known what was happening to her? Mike hoped not. The amount of alcohol she had consumed would have made it very easy for the killer.

Easy for Theo too, he hoped.

Fact number two had taken everyone by surprise. It seemed that, murdered or not, Theo could have expected little more time on this earth. She had a massive and malignant tumour behind the posterior lobe of her liver. Her body was riddled with secondary infection. Theo had been dying.

He had returned to her house looking for medication. There had been none.

He had chosen not to bring David Martin in for questioning that night. The evidence against him was, at best, circumstantial and, besides, Mike felt that if he didn't get some rest soon he'd be sleeping on his feet.

Even more strange, perhaps, was the reaction of Theo's doctor. He'd been informed of her death, of course, but when Mike called him he professed ignorance of Theo's condition. So concerned was he that his memory might be failing him that he had checked through Theo's record.

'No,' he said. 'I'm glad to say dementia isn't setting in. Theodora Howard has seen me only three times in the past year. Once for a sprained ankle. Once for a throat infection, oh, and the third time I told her that she had a rather virulent influenza virus. That one was a call out. She'd been up all night with sickness and a high temperature and someone had got worried. I've a note here that I was called out by her lodger. Would that make sense?'

But surely, Mike had asked, she must have been in pain. She must have been diagnosed. She must have known.

The doctor had just shaken his head. 'I've not seen Miss Howard in the last six months,' he said. 'If she knew, if she was receiving medication, well, it wasn't from me.'

Mike had spoken to John Tynan a couple of hours before, filling him in on the bare facts, aware that waiting for news was putting a great strain on the older man. He was glad that Maria was there.

Fact number three, Theo must have started drinking from the moment she had walked through the door. A neighbour had seen her come home at about five o'clock. She had parked her car easily enough in the small space left in front of the house, so it seemed a fair bet that she was still sober. Davy claimed to have found the body at about twenty to eight. The boy had been seen running away about thirty minutes before. All in all, Theo must have died some time between five and, say, seven-thirty.

The pathologist's estimate based on body temperature couldn't put it much more accurately than that, the best guess being about seven o'clock. And that made sense. She'd need time to have drunk so much.

Arriving at John's house he cut the car engine, sitting back in his seat for a few moments to gather his thoughts before going inside. Maria was right, he thought. He would have to change his old car. He'd just been putting it off for far too long. Driving hers was a sheer delight and one less thing to worry about. Twice now, his had died on him. Once at a set of traffic lights when he'd already been late for a meeting and once in the middle of nowhere. He'd had to get it towed to a garage.

He got out of the car, aware that the front door was open and John was waving to him.

'Phone call for you,' John shouted.

'Oh God, what now?'

He hurried into the hall, pausing to kiss Maria on the cheek as he passed her by.

'Croft.' He listened in silence, then thanked the speaker and put the receiver down.

'Well?' Maria asked him.

'That was Price. There's been an odd development in the Theo Howard case.'

'One you haven't told us yet?' John said gruffly. 'I thought we'd had enough surprises for one night.'

'So did I. Price has just got off the phone with a Detective Inspector Charles Morrow. Based at Devizes in Wiltshire.'

'Wiltshire, what's that got to do with Theo?'

'That's just it, we don't know. But it seems he's been heading up a murder enquiry. The body's only just been identified and Morrow was going through the woman's effects. Theo Howard's telephone number was among them.'

9 p.m.

It had taken a lot of ringing around and more than a few threats, but Phil Myers had finally got the location of the party his daughter was supposed to be going to.

Paula Myers was outraged. 'She told me she was going to the pictures and staying over at her friend's afterwards.' She looked at her husband, anxiety replacing anger. 'You don't seriously think she'll turn up there, do you?'

'I don't know. But her friends must be able to tell me something.' He paused, then got up and resumed his earlier pacing around the room like a trapped animal. 'I can't believe she'd go off like this. Just go. I mean, if she had problems I could understand it, but . . . why couldn't she just talk to us?'

Paula's eyes focused on him and she shook her head. 'When was the last time either of us could talk to you without getting our heads bitten off?' she said. 'You've built a wall so high round yourself we can't even see you these days, never mind try to talk.'

She could see him bristling with anger, ready to resume the fight that had raged off and on all night and most of the day. Paula didn't think she could take any more of it. Instead, she shook her head, lifting tired hands to rub her face as though scrubbing it clean.

'No, no. It wasn't just you. Neither of us really asked her anything, did we? It was always "How was school, Sarah? Do you have any homework, Sarah? Do you really think you can make up good enough grades at that ordinary school, Sarah?" My God, I'd listen to us sometimes and I'd want to switch off too. No wonder she didn't talk to us.'

'We weren't that bad!' He crossed to the table and sat down opposite. For a moment she thought that he would reach across and take her hand, but he didn't.

He said, 'We care about her, that's all. Is that so wrong?'

'No, of course not, but – I don't know, maybe we were so busy trying to get it right we forgot why we were doing it?'

He got up and went through to the hall. She could
hear him, visualize him taking his coat from the hook
and looking in the hall mirror to straighten his tie. Then
she heard the front door slam.

Chapter Sixteen

9.10 p.m.

The Parishes had gone away for the weekend leaving their two teenage sons behind. The oldest was nineteen and the youngest in the same year as his Sarah. Phillip Myers had worked this out from the assorted bits and pieces of information he had gleaned from Sarah's friends.

The Parishes' house was a nineteen-thirties bay-fronted semi at the end of a quiet cul-de-sac. He had not been able to find out the number. The kids he'd talked to knew where it was, but not unimportant details like addresses. He had hoped there would be evidence of a party going on, remembering, with a guilty start, the parties of his late teenage years. The complaints of neighbours. The desperate efforts to clean up before parents got back. The housewarming when he'd moved into his first bedsit flat and, long before independence, that one, humiliating time when the police had been called to a friend's place because of the noise and someone hadn't been smart enough to flush their stash down the toilet in time. He still remembered the horror of having to explain to his folks why he hadn't been home all night.

'But I was older,' he told himself. 'I was a student then.'

And yes, he had been, all of two years Sarah's senior. Somehow, in the drive over to the Parishes' house, that two years had ceased to be such a great divide. Now all he wanted was to get his daughter back.

The cul-de-sac was so quiet he thought he had to be mistaken, or that his informants had deliberately misled him. He drove slowly to the end of the road. Two houses stood together. No car in the drive of one, and lights on in the front room and the front bedroom. The other house appeared to be in darkness.

He got out of the car and looked around. The cul-de-sac was empty. The rain had ceased to fall and now the wind was rising, blowing the clouds across the moon. Lights glowed behind closed curtains, television pictures flickered across uncurtained glass. Phillip began to walk towards the semi at the end. Dimly through the thickly curtained bay window of the house, he could hear music.

His footsteps were loud on the gravel of the drive. Phillip stood for a moment in front of the wooden door. What if she wasn't here? Was it really likely that she would be?

He raised his fist and began to hammer on the door.

Phillip Myers had lost his temper. Lost it in a big way and even by the time Price arrived had not yet fully recovered it.

Phillip had not bothered with introductions. As soon as the door opened, he had pushed his way into the house, marched into the front room from which the music was escaping and turned off the CD player.

The silence was absolute within seconds. Then broken as the protests began.

'Oh come on, man, we weren't making that much noise . . .'

'I'm here to find my daughter,' Phillip announced loudly. 'Some of you, one of you has got to know where she is and you're going to tell me. You're going to tell me now.'

Graham, the eldest Parish son, stepped forward, still sober enough to put two and two together and not wanting anything to spoil his show. He tried to be placatory.

'You must be Sarah's dad. Look, I'm sorry, mate, but she's not here.'

Phillip turned on his heel and walked from the room, calling Sarah's name.

'Look, we told you, she ain't here.'

'Sarah!'

Phillip pushed into the kitchen, opening doors, shouting loudly as he did so.

'Sarah. I know you're here, Sarah!'

He stormed up the stairs, shoving anyone aside who got in his way.

'She isn't here! Look, mate, if you don't get out of here, I'm going to call the police.'

Graham raced up the stairs after him. He grabbed Phillip's arm as he reached the top of the stairs preparing to search the bedrooms, the bathroom, even the attic if there was a chance Sarah might be hiding there.

As Graham reached out and touched Phillip's sleeve the man turned on him, jerking his arm aside, hitting out reflexively with his other fist. He missed the young man by a mile, but his fist made contact with the landing window. Glass shattered, breaking the silence outside.

Thrown aside by Phillip's sudden movement, Graham lost balance. Arms flailing, he toppled backwards down the stairs.

A girl began to scream. People were dashing in all directions. Some to help Graham, some scattering away from Phillip Myers and others leaping forward to try to restrain him. Amidst the chaos, someone had the presence of mind to call the police.

Price was not amused. He had been about to go home when he was told Phillip Myers had been arrested.

He was even less amused now, an hour and a half later, having seen Myers' hand patched up by the duty surgeon and spent a further forty minutes with him in the interview room getting his version of what was going on.

'Look, Mr Myers,' he said at last. 'We're all sympathetic. We all know what you must be going through, but if you had information you should have passed it on. Then we could have checked out this party, made sure your daughter wasn't there without all this unpleasantness.'

Phillip Myers looked at him, a cold anger in his eyes. 'I want to find my daughter, Sergeant. I want her back home safe and, frankly, I don't give a damn who I upset or how much "unpleasantness" I cause doing it. And as to calling you lot in, one thing I have learnt, Sergeant Price, is just how bloody little use that would be.'

He stood up and began to move towards the door. 'I'm leaving now. I've got more important things to do.'

Price got to his feet also, the officer sitting near the door moving to block Myers' exit.

'Sit down, Mr Myers. I said, *sit down*!'

Reluctantly, his gaze drifting from one to the other of the two men, Myers sat.

'Now listen to me. You were brought here on an assault charge. If you keep pushing we'll add breach of the peace to that and you'll be spending the night in the cells, and with the crowd we've got in here tonight, you'll be spending it up to your armpits in piss and puke. I have had about two hours' sleep in the last two days and, frankly, the sympathy angle is wearing just a little thin. As it happens, Graham Parish hasn't said yet that he wants to press charges. He's being understanding, which, in his position, is a darn sight more than I would be. You want to think yourself lucky that Mr Parish bounced or you'd find yourself up in court on Monday morning with a count of GBH on your record.'

He paused to draw breath, and, seeing that Myers was about to start again, held up a hand to silence him.

'That's enough. Now get off home. If we or Graham Parish, or his parents for that matter, decide to press charges then we know where to find you, don't we?'

Phillip stood up and walked stiffly towards the door. 'My car?' he said.

'Is where you left it. I suggest you take a cab.'

Price sat for several minutes after Myers left. He was thinking deeply. Myers had never really explained the

111

scratch marks on his face and he had shown tonight that he was capable of violence.

He shook his head. It was hardly the same. A flailing attack against a young man who'd got him riled was hardly the same as deliberate sexual assaults on girls as young as his own daughter.

Price gave that some more thought. Sexual violence? Was that why Sarah had run away...? It was worth following up. At this point in time, anything seemed worth following up.

11.30 p.m.

The woman had dark hair and deep blue eyes. He'd been with her before, many times, and always there had been a pleasing simplicity to their lovemaking.

She had a good body, strong and supple and infinitely satisfying. Her mouth and hands soft and warm, and what she might be lacking in skill she made up for in familiarity and a willingness to please.

'Will you be gone again when I wake up?' Her voice sleepy and content.

'I don't know. Perhaps I'll stay.'

She smiled then and stretched luxuriously, turning on her side before going to sleep.

There had been only two women in his life who had ever behaved that way, been so relaxed and fearless in his presence. So unconcerned and unworried about appearance. And the other was dead now.

He swung his legs over the side of the bed and

switched on the television set. The hotel had satellite and he flicked aimlessly through the channels. He kept the sound turned down, the woman's soft breathing the only noise in the room.

He found himself listening closely to the sound. Hearing her every breath, in and out, slower and deeper, deeper. He found himself breathing in time with her, matching her rhythm, his own breath slow and deep, a sleeping, dying breath.

What if it stopped, what if he slowed his own breathing, caught her rhythm, made it his own and then made it stop?

It never ceased to fascinate, this fine line between what was living and what was not.

This woman lived; the other one did not. There had been that final moment when the breath was no longer breath and the something that set her apart from death was gone for ever.

He sat for a minute longer, watching the woman sleep, waiting for the moment when he might decide if she should live or she should die.

Then he sighed, gave up the game and began to dress. He took his cheque book from the inside pocket of his coat and wrote a cheque, leaving it on the dressing-table weighted down by the glass ashtray.

He left so silently the woman would not wake.

Walking swiftly down the hall.

Remembering to breathe.

Chapter Seventeen

11.40 p.m.

Jake had returned home and gone straight down to the basement. He could hear the man crying as he went through the second room. He'd been struggling to free himself and had fallen off the bed. He had stayed where he fell, lying at an awkward angle with his face pressed against the bare floor.

Jake had not had time to change for the benefit of the camera this time. He was dressed casually in jeans and open-necked white shirt. But he took time to don the ski mask before dragging his victim by pinioned arms and dumping him back on to the bed. The man screamed in agony as he hauled already cramped and swollen limbs back against the joints.

'Where did you think you could get to?' Jake asked him gently. 'No one leaves here walking, you know, my friend. No one.'

'Please. Let me go. I don't know who you are. I haven't even seen your face. I wouldn't tell anyone. Not a soul. I swear it, on my mother's life, I swear it. I haven't even seen your face . . .'

For a moment Jake paused, bending over him, smiling behind the mask. Then slowly, and with infinite care, he pulled the tape from the man's eyes. They struggled open, lashes fighting the adhesive left from the tape and the sudden blinding brightness. Jake stepped back out of shot and removed his mask.

Sunday,
18 December

Chapter Eighteen

9 a.m.

Mike put the phone down and returned to the breakfast table. 'That was Price,' he said. 'Checking in before he leaves for Devizes. He's dropping in on the Myers on the way out. It seems they called demanding to see him. He's going straight from there.'

'Anything new?' John enquired.

'Beyond the fact that David Martin appears to have done a moonlight, no.'

'David? What do you mean?'

'I mean he's left the hotel. He left a cheque in his room for payment of the bill and phoned them this morning to say he'd checked out. They called us. Apparently, he slipped out through the back way at some point last night.' He paused. 'It doesn't look good, John.'

Tynan sighed. 'Stupid fool,' he said. 'No, you're right. It's hardly a good way to proclaim his innocence. But I still find it hard to believe he could have harmed Theo. It just doesn't feel right.'

'What's this, cop instinct?' Maria asked. She smiled. 'I know, John. Maybe he'll come to his senses and turn himself in.'

The morning papers crashed through the letter box. Mike was closest to the door and went to get them. He scanned the front page as he walked back into the kitchen.

Two stories competed for front-page space: an update on the sex attacker following the printing of the letters and the report on Sarah's disappearance from the leisure centre. The report kept to the broad lines of the release put out by the police press office. It was accompanied by photographs of the missing girl and an appeal by Mrs Myers for her daughter to come home. 'There's nothing we can't sort out,' the woman said. 'Nothing that can't be put right.'

There was, Mike noted, no mention of the girl having her mother's Visa card.

He dropped the paper on to the kitchen table and continued with his breakfast.

9.30 a.m.

The path to the Myers' house was original to the building. Black, white and red tiles laid out in an ornate geometric design. It was also well worn and, in the pouring rain, treacherously slippery as Sergeant Price ran towards the front door.

Paula Myers opened it as he reached the step. Price stood in the hall, wiping his feet energetically on the doormat.

'She has a boyfriend,' Paula Myers announced, with as much horror, Price thought, as if she'd just found her daughter mainlining drugs.

'Well,' Price countered, 'she's of the age when girls often do.'

'She has no time for boyfriends.' Phillip Myers

emerged from the dining-room. 'Sarah's studies are what's important right now. I want her to get somewhere in life, not—'

'Quite, sir.' Price cut him off mid-flow. 'Look,' he said, more than a little annoyed. 'You got me out here on what you said was an urgent call. Made it sound as though you'd had contact with Sarah at the very least. You can sort out your differences with your daughter later. What's more important is does the boyfriend know where Sarah is?'

Myers stared, then shook his head and sank down into one of the high-backed chairs that stood either side of the dining-room door. He looked tired and suddenly quite grey. It was, Price thought, the first real emotion he had yet seen Myers display.

'Have you spoken to the boyfriend, Mr Myers, Mrs Myers?'

'No. No, that's just it,' Paula Myers told him. 'We found out from one of her friends, Maddie. She didn't want to tell, but I suppose she was more worried about Sarah than about what we might think.' She glanced meaningfully at her husband, who looked away, angrily. 'She gave us his name, Terry. Terry Ryan. He lives on Cavendish Road, right around the corner. But we don't know where . . .'

Her face crumpled suddenly and she began to cry, very softly as though embarrassed. 'We were going to knock on doors. Ask if anyone knew him.' She looked up at Price as though waiting for him to sort it. He reached out and patted her awkwardly on the shoulder.

'It's all right,' he said. 'We'll find him and I'll call you the moment we have any news.'

She nodded bleakly, seemed to be waiting for him to leave before she completely broke down. Her husband sat still, gazing at the floor.

'I'll call you, straight away,' Price reiterated, then tugged the front door open and stepped out into the rain.

It hadn't taken long to trace Terrence James Ryan. A call back to divisional to get them to check the voters' register and he had the address of Judith Ryan, Flat 2, on the top floor of a converted house at the end of Cavendish Road.

Price drove around the corner from Sullivan Avenue. The cordon was still up around the Howard home, but there was no one on the door. Retreated inside, no doubt, out of the foul weather. It was wrong, he thought, what they said about lightning not striking in the same place; the Howard house practically backed on to the Myers' garden.

The address he wanted was at the other end of Cavendish Road. A tall, imposing house, similar in design to the Myers', but this had a neglected, run-down look to it. Paint peeling from the front door and rust from the iron railing that blocked off the basement flat, staining the pavement.

There were five names, written in faded ink behind a perspex panel. No doorbell and no security. The door opened easily by an external handle, stairs straight ahead of him. Two doors leading off the hall, one to his left and one at the end of the hall. Both had Yale locks and doorbells.

Letters from the previous morning post lay unsorted on a narrow table. Price leafed through them. Mainly bills and circulars; nothing for Judith Ryan or her son.

Price glanced back at the front door. Not exactly the most security-conscious of places he'd ever been in.

The stairs were thinly carpeted and the polish on the wooden banister had more to do with the rub of hands than regular cleaning. There was grey-blue paint over faded wallpaper on the dusty walls.

Judith Ryan's flat was on the second floor with a small rug spelling 'Welcome' set outside. Price knocked and rang the bell, holding it down for the count of five before letting go. The door was opened as he took his finger away and a red-haired woman who looked too young to have a teenage son stared out at him. Her eyes were red too, Price noticed, and she looked as though she'd had little sleep.

Price had his identification in his hand. 'Police,' he said. 'I'm . . .'

'It's Terry, isn't it? You've found him. What's happened? Please, he is all right?'

Price was taken aback for an instant, then he caught on. 'Terry's missing?' he said.

Judith looked blank. 'I thought that must be why you'd come?' she said. 'I mean, you see, it's not like him.' She took a deep breath. 'Terry didn't come home on Friday night.'

Jane Adams

9.30 a.m.

Max Harriman was reading the morning paper. Looking at the image of Sarah Myers on the front page it crossed his mind that this might be one of Jake's; she certainly had the blonde looks and slightly innocent air that Jake was specializing in at the moment, like a younger version of what Marion had become.

Max frowned slightly at the memory. Marion had not been good for Jake. Max had known, from the moment Jake had become so excited about those pictures Vincenza had sent him, that Marion would not be good for him.

It was true, Marion had inspired some of Jake's most beautiful work, some of his most original stuff, especially in the final scenes – Max couldn't wait to see that final film – but she had involved Jake much too closely, made him think of her as something more than just another star. It had become personal and that was always a mistake.

Max sighed and shook his head. In one thing, one perception, he was well ahead of Jake. Max had learnt long ago that their type, people like himself and Jake, they weren't made for the settled life with the one-to-one commitments that went with it. It didn't do to get involved like that, it took away so much of your objectivity.

To be a great artist, Jake had once said, you have to be both passionate and detached about your creativity. It had been a great phrase, Max thought. The local press had thought so too. And it should have been good –

it had taken Jake all day to think of it and not exactly been the easiest of speeches to slip into the conversation.

Max put his paper down and riffled through the stack of cuttings books stacked on the floor. He knew just where to find the piece he wanted, flipping open the page to show a picture of two teenage boys grinning out at the photographer and the single paragraph beside it describing the award that they had won.

The headline spoke of 'Budding Film-makers' winning a top award and went on to tell how Jake Bowen and Nick Jarvis had won second place in a national competition for young film-makers – documentary section – for a film made about a local factory strike.

Nicholas Jarvis. It was a very long time since anyone had called him that.

He looked closely at the two boys. Excited smiles, lousy haircuts, standing on the steps of the terraced house belonging to Jake's parents.

They had been fifteen years old. The camera borrowed by their English teacher from a local community group. The teacher had fussed and nagged the whole time they were making their film, Max remembered. Always getting in the way.

Max smiled. Life had seemed so full of possibilities even then.

9.40 a.m.

Mike was still at John Tynan's when Stacey rang the police station. The memory had come to her in a dream,

125

and for a little while after waking she had lain still and thought about it. Trying to fit the dream memory into what she knew to be real.

Painfully, she re-ran the entire thing, from her storming away from Richard to the moment he had found her and driven her attacker away.

The tightness in her chest, the panic that this evoked was almost more than she could bear, but she knew that what she thought she remembered could be crucial. She had to go through it, sort it out.

Finally, she sat up in bed and pushed the covers aside. The telephone was downstairs in the living-room. Stacey pulled on her dressing-gown and made her way down, repeating the words in her head as though they might escape her again.

This was no dream. Stacey was certain of that now. The words had come hard on the heels of a dream, but they had come into her mind in that time between sleep and waking and now she had prodded the memory, felt the pain of it, she knew that it was real.

Her mother called to her from the kitchen as she went by. Walked silently past her father as he came into the hall. Made her way straight to the telephone and dialled the number on the card that she had been given.

She was startled to find that Mike wasn't there.

'Oh!' Stacey said. 'Well, look, can you get a message to him, get him to phone me? It is important, yes. Tell him it's Stacey. Stacey Holmes. And that I've remembered something.'

Chapter Nineteen

10 a.m.

'Do you mind if I smoke?'

Price shrugged. 'It's your house.'

'I know, but some people don't like it. Terry doesn't, I tend not to when he's here.'

Price smiled. 'Difficult things, teenagers,' he said. 'Think they can tell you everything.'

'Do you have children?'

Price shook his head. 'No, not me, never found anyone daft enough to have them with me.'

There was silence for a moment or two, then Price said, 'You reported him missing Friday night? You got a visit, I presume?'

'Yeah, a young constable. A quarter past one, it was.' She smiled. 'He looked a bit lost himself; funny, you know what they say about policemen getting younger . . .'

She trailed off, looking away from him and taking a cigarette from the pack. Her hands trembled a little as she lit the match. She was, Price thought, holding herself together very well now that he was here, but the pale face and red-rimmed eyes told a different story.

'I thought you'd come to tell me something,' she said. 'I thought . . .'

'No, like I said, I didn't even know your son had

gone missing. Uniform deals with most of the Mispas, the older ones anyway.'

'Mispas?'

'Missing persons. Sorry. You see, when they get to Terry's age and there's nothing suspicious, well, the thing is, most of them go off in a strop and turn up again the next day. Starving hungry and ready for another round of parent-baiting.'

He watched her closely, not certain he was taking the right road with her, but she smiled slightly. 'Yeah, I suppose you're right,' she said. 'I mean, Terry's not a baby, but he is my son and he's never done anything like this before, you see. And it wasn't like we'd argued or anything. I saw him go off to school on Friday morning and he was fine. He was just fine.' The tears were back, threatening to overflow as she blinked rapidly.

'This girl, the one that's missing too. Sarah. It wasn't uniform that dealt with her?' She looked up sharply at him, the unspoken accusation clear. Was this girl more important than her son?

'Yes, it was. As I told you, she went to let someone into her mother's aerobics class and never came back. There was a worry at the time that she might be another victim . . .'

'Of this sex attacker?'

'Yes. You see I've been involved in working on that one. She fitted the profile, fifteen years old, small and blonde.'

'But Terry doesn't even know this girl,' Judith argued. The protest faded as soon as it was made and she sighed, 'He never mentioned her.' She shook her head.

Suddenly she sounded angry, frustrated. Price probed carefully, sensing that there was something more than just a son careless of what he told his mother.

'Did he talk much about his friends?'

'Of course he did!'

Obviously he'd touched a raw nerve. She recovered herself immediately, consciously. 'No, not really. I mean, we haven't lived here all that long, five, six months or so. And it's not, well, not the sort of place you bring friends back to . . .'

'I think it's very nice.' Price looked around at the poorly furnished flat. 'You've done a lot to make it homely,' he said gently and found that he really meant it. There wasn't much in the flat that hadn't come from a second-hand shop or cheap discount store, but the walls had been colour-washed and rag-rolled and finished with a pretty border. There were books and magazines and flowers in a cheap glass vase. An effort to make the place like home. But he could see she might feel sensitive, and if she had known about Sarah, known about the way she lived . . . The Myers house might be only round the corner but it could just as well have been a world away. It could have been a reason for Terry not to mention her, if he knew how his mother felt.

'And he never mentioned Sarah?' Price asked her again.

'No, I told you. He never did.' She hesitated, then said, 'You see, Terry and I, I guess we were getting to know each other again. I'd got divorced, you see, and Terry didn't live with me for quite a while.'

Price waited. There was more, but he clearly wasn't

going to get it now. He got up ready to go. Terry had no local family, she had said. No family at all, in fact. Except his grandparents, her parents, and they'd just moved abroad. No friends he might have gone to, nowhere to go.

Judith had seemed awkward and uncomfortable then. It was as though she had suddenly realized how little she knew about her son and she was shaken by the knowledge.

She'd get back to him, Price thought, when she'd had another chance to think it through.

'I'll call you as soon as I know anything,' he said, as he had done with the Myers a short time before.

'The hall phone doesn't always work,' she said, 'and I don't have one. Not here.'

'Ah, right. I see.' That explained why Mr Myers hadn't been able to trace Judith himself. He'd make bets that Myers would have made a beeline for the phone book the moment he had Terry's name.

He took a plain white card from his pocket and scribbled his name and number on it. As an afterthought he added DI Mike Croft's as well. 'He's my boss,' he said. 'Give me a call if Terry gets in touch.'

She took the card and nodded, tears beginning again as he took his leave.

Price walked back down the four flights of stairs and let himself out of the front door. There was something very wrong with this whole scenario, he thought. He just wished that he could work out what.

10.15 a.m.

Stacey's message was phoned through to Mike at John Tynan's cottage.

'She didn't say what she had remembered?' he reiterated.

'No, sir, insisted on talking to you. Shame to spoil your day off though. We could send a uniform round.'

'No, no, I'll go to see her. You said there was something about the missing girl?'

'Yes. A bus driver called it in. He'd just picked up his morning paper and recognized the girl. He's sure he dropped her off at Hoton about ten o'clock last night.'

'At Hoton? He's certain?'

'Seems so.'

'No more news on David Martin, I suppose?'

There was not. Mike hung up thoughtfully.

'Hoton?' Maria asked him.

'Our runaway. A bus driver thinks he remembers dropping her off there about ten o'clock last night.' He glanced at his watch. 'I have to go, I'm afraid, see this girl, Stacey.'

'Right. Look, I'll head back to Oaklands, I'll give you a call later.'

Stacey told him about her dream that was not a dream. She went through it calmly and in careful detail. She might, Mike thought, have been describing a shopping trip or her holiday plans, until you looked at the way her hands were shaking.

'And you're sure that's what he said?'

'Quite sure, Inspector Croft.' She took a deep breath and said the words again. 'He said, "I know you want it, Marion. I know you do. I know you do." '

Her words were flat, deliberately devoid of all feeling or tone.

'And the name was Marion. Not Mary or Marie or anything similar? You're absolutely certain about that?'

Stacey nodded. 'It's not a common name,' she said. 'I mean I know two Maries and even a Mary, though she's older than me. But Marion. I don't think I've ever even met a Marion. So I know I've got it right.'

Mike thanked her and got up to go.

'Do you think it will help you?' Stacey asked him.

He nodded. 'Yes, I really think it might. As you say, Marion isn't that common a name. It could be very significant. And I want you to know, I think you're handling this brilliantly.'

She half-smiled at him. 'I don't feel brilliant,' she said. 'Only I keep telling myself, he didn't really hurt me and I wasn't raped. Not like those other girls. I keep telling myself that.'

Mike left her, his mind a turmoil of possibilities.

No, Marion was not a particularly common name. Unusual enough to be distinctive. And he could not help but make the connection. Marion had been the name of the woman whose death Price was now following up, and Marion O'Donnel had Theo Howard's number in her book.

3 p.m.

John Tynan was astonished to find David Martin on his doorstep.

'You've got to let me in, John. I have to talk to someone.'

'How about talking to the police?' John questioned. 'They're looking for you.'

Davy shook his head. 'I know, at least, I guessed they must be.'

John Tynan looked thoughtfully at the young man standing on his doorstep. He was unshaven and rumpled; his clothes looked as though he'd slept in them. Very different from the smartly dressed figure John had usually seen at Theo's.

'You'd better come inside,' he said. 'But I'm warning you, David, when you've talked to me, I'm taking you into Norwich. You've got to turn yourself in.'

'You going to make me?' For a moment, John thought he was going to hit out at him. Then he shook his head. 'No, you're right. I've got to go back and I know that. But I've spent all night going through this. I needed time. And I need to talk to someone first.' He gave John a look of such desperation that the older man was moved, despite his instinct towards caution.

Tynan said, 'See it from their point of view. From mine. Theo is found dead, murdered in her own home. You disappear, no word of explanation, you just skip out through the back way like some common thief. And you ask us not to think badly of you? For all I know, you might well have killed Theo. For all the police

133

know, you probably did.' He shook his head. 'You've got half an hour, Davy. Long enough to have a cup of tea and give me your version of events before I drive you to the station. Talk to me and let me take you in and I'll do everything I can for you. But you run out again and there'll be no one believes you're not implicated. You must see that.'

David nodded. 'Yes, I do. I do. Thank you, you won't regret it. I promise you that.'

Chapter Twenty

It had been a long drive but the light was already fading when Price arrived. Morrow suggested they go straight out and view the crime scene while there was still daylight left to see. Dental records had provided the final confirmation that the body was that of Marion O'Donnel.

Morrow drove. An experience Price vowed he was never going to repeat, tearing along the curving downland road as though it was a slalom course grafted on to a race track.

He pulled the car into a farm gate close to a small cottage and pointed.

'Up there, that's where we found her. The gate was opened. Somebody had cut through the chain.'

'They came prepared then,' Price commented as he climbed out of the car, trying not to notice that his legs were shaking from all the compensatory braking he'd been doing.

Charlie Morrow nodded. 'Oh yes,' he said, 'I think they came prepared.'

The place where the car had burned was the widest point of the track, before it narrowed into a single file walkway between the fields. It was unremarkable, just a barren area of rutted mud and grass and a rough oblong of charred earth showing where the car had stood.

Morrow had talked almost non-stop during their

135

drive, bringing Price up to speed on his conversation with Mike. He had, Price discovered, a disconcerting way of turning to look at his passenger while he talked rather than concentrating on the road. Price was certain he'd made most of the curves on a mixture of memory and instinct. It certainly hadn't been by sight.

He flipped through the photographs of the crime scene that Morrow had provided for him, trying to match the pictures to the reality. The photographs showed what must have been a wet, foul-tempered night; they revealed little of the surrounding landscape.

'What's that over there?' he asked, his attention attracted by a large conical hump that rose out of the flat earth on the opposite side of the road.

'Silbury Hill,' Morrow told him. 'I'll take you up there later, when you've more chance of getting a view. It's fenced off now, problems of erosion, but we still get the odd tourist braving the barbed wire, looking for crop circles or something equally psychic I suppose.'

'You're not into that sort of thing, then?' Price grinned wryly.

Charlie Morrow grunted. 'Not so's you'd notice,' he said. He gestured towards the rise behind them. 'Want to go and take a look?'

He set off up the path without waiting for a reply.

Price followed.

It seemed an oddly appropriate place to contemplate a murder, Price thought. The mist was coming down, much as it must have done the evening that the woman died, and it would soon be dark. The dampness seeped through his clothes and into his bones, but he hardly noticed it. Despite himself, he was captivated.

Morrow had led him into the tomb itself. West Kennet Long Barrow. Thousands of years old, and Price could feel the weight of every one of them pressing down on him through what looked like precariously balanced rock.

Someone had lit candles inside the tomb. He commented on them.

'People come here all the time,' Morrow told him. 'Religious feelings they're supposed to have for it or something.'

He sounded dismissive, but there was something in his voice that made Price look at him suspiciously. It was at least an edge of affection; it might even have been a touch of awe.

It was in the tomb and the flickering candlelight that Morrow, with an unexpected sense of the dramatic, gave Price the two sheets of folded paper.

One was the poem Price already knew, a copy of the one found in Theo Howard's hand.

'It was in the dead woman's flat,' Morrow told him. 'Is it the same?'

Price nodded slowly. 'The other one was found in her bag. It seems to be about this place.'

He unfolded the paper and began to read.

'I spent the night beneath the stones,
he said,
But didn't sleep,

Jane Adams

Their whisperings kept my thoughts alive,
And held my mind from dreams.

I spent the night beneath the stones
          he said
And watched the beacon lit
          upon the dead man's hill.
And when the night had fallen full,
I spent the night beneath the stones,
          he said

I spent the night beneath the stones,
          he said,
     But did not sleep.
     Your voice within the beacon
          kept my thoughts alive.
     And held my mind from dreams.

At the bottom of the sheet were written the words, 'With love, David.'

Chapter Twenty-One

5 p.m.

Harriman was preparing his evening meal. He took chicken breast from the styrofoam package with an old fork he kept specifically for meat and placed it on a grill lined with foil. Potatoes were already baking in the tiny oven; he had to turn the flame up high to get the skins to crisp the way he liked. He had already prepared the salad, slicing everything neatly and arranging carefully on his plate.

Max liked to cook. He knew his workmates had found it a little odd when he'd admitted to this in an unguarded moment, but the fact was, it gave him great satisfaction that he knew exactly what went into his body.

His mother had always cooked, drumming into him from an early age how important it was to treat your body right, and Max had taken her advice to heart. He kept himself fit with regular exercise, his body well fed and his mind active, and he was meticulous about the details.

Max crossed to the sink and washed his hands once again. The third time during his ritual of food preparation.

Then he examined his hands and nails with the greatest care.

Max did a manual job operating a lathe, and the

hands of his fellow workers were calloused and stained in a way that Max could not allow. He wore gloves at work and kept his hands very clean at other times. In addition, twice daily he massaged them with a cream used, so the advertising said, by Icelandic fishermen to combat the effects of cold.

It had earned him some odd comments the first few weeks at this job, but he did his work well enough to silence the criticism and the 'he's a bloody poof' jokes had faded when they had spotted the pictures taped to the inside of his locker.

It was, Max thought, the sort of thing that Jake would do to throw others off the track. The women he attacked would remember his hands as being soft and smooth – if they remembered anything at all – not rough and hard like the skilled manual worker that he was.

He went back to the sink and scrubbed at his nails once again, shaking his head. There were still marks. Stains around the nails and on his knuckles, but it would have to do.

He thought of Jake. Jake had never laughed at his neatness or his meticulous habits. Jake had been the only one Max's mother had ever really liked, but then, Jake always knew the right thing to say.

Staring at the table with its blue checked cloth, carefully set and clean enough for his mother to be proud of, Max remembered how it had been when Jake had come to call for him.

'Your house, it always looks so nice,' Jake would say, and Max's mother would award him one of her small, tight smiles and let Max go out without another word.

Max's face grew dark as another image imprinted across the first. His mother dead on the kitchen floor, her small, tight smile replaced by a bloody grin that split across her cheeks from ear to ear.

5.15 p.m.

Judith had walked for a long time before finally getting up enough courage to go to the Myers' house. Their number was in the phone book and had taken only moments to find. The house was only a ten-minute walk from her flat, but it had been close on an hour before Judith had finally been able to bring herself to go to the door.

Paula Myers replied quickly to her ring, her pale face anxious and the faint hopefulness in her eyes fading as she saw the stranger on her doorstep. She had been expecting news. Judith didn't look like news.

'Yes,' she said. 'Can I help you?'

Judith swallowed nervously. 'I'm sorry,' she said. 'Sorry to bother you. It's just that I thought maybe we should talk; if we put our heads together, we may get some idea.' She broke off, aware of how jumbled her words must sound and of the woman's cold stare.

She began again. 'I'm . . . I'm Judith Ryan,' she explained. 'Terry's mother. I just wondered, have you heard anything?'

For a moment Judith thought Paula Myers was going to fly at her, the look of rage and pain that crossed her face was so strong and so obvious. Then it faded. The two women gazed at one another with red-rimmed eyes.

'I think you'd better come in,' Paula said.

'It's a lovely house,' Judith said. She was seated at the kitchen table cradling a mug of very hot coffee between her hands.

'Thank you. You live on Cavendish Road . . . it's a nice road, Cavendish.'

Judith half-smiled. 'We live at the other end, in one of those tall three-storey places. It's flats now. Terry and I, we have the top floor.' She sipped her coffee. 'It's all right really, and it's our own place. That's what matters.'

Paula didn't really know what to say to this woman now she was inside the house. They had spent the last ten minutes like this. Dodging around the questions each one wanted to ask. Trying not to step on feelings that were so bruised already one more hurt would make little difference.

'I didn't know about Terry,' she said.

'No, neither did I. I mean about Sarah. He never told me.' Judith hesitated. 'I thought we'd got a good relationship,' she said. 'Thought he told me things. But he never mentioned Sarah. He didn't mention many of his friends really, but I never noticed somehow. Not till now.' She smiled wryly, trying not to feel too uncomfortable with the admission.

Paula smiled back. 'Nice to know we're not the only ones facing that conclusion,' she said. 'God, but I feel so helpless just sitting here. Maybe Phil was right, at least he did something.'

'Did something?'

'Yes, well, it turns out they were going to a party yesterday. Both of them.'

'Terry as well? He didn't say a thing. Well, he talked about going out . . .'

'Oh, don't fret. Sarah spun a yarn about staying at a friend's. Seemed to think we'd disapprove if she'd told the truth.'

'Would you?'

'No! Of course not. Sarah's . . . Probably. I mean yes. I suppose we would if I'd thought she planned to be out all night. Anyway, Phil found out where this party was supposed to be. His going round there didn't do much at the time, but this morning one of the girls phoned us. Said, did we know about Terry?' She paused, smiled grimly. 'The parents are away, where this party was, so you can just imagine.' She smiled bitterly. 'I mean that's just it, isn't it? You can just imagine, more to the point you can remember.'

Judith thought back to her rather strict upbringing. Actually parties at sixteen without adults present were not something in her experience, but there had been other things that probably more than made up for that.

'But I mean, we could have compromised. Picked her up at midnight or something. I don't know. And it doesn't explain why they ran away.' She looked awkwardly at Judith. 'I'm sorry to ask this, but was Terry in some kind of trouble or worried about something? I mean, I know how that must sound . . .'

Judith was shaking her head. 'No. I'm certain not. He was happy here. Settled well in school. It had been a fresh start for us.' She sighed deeply. 'I don't know why he would go off like that.' She looked hopefully at Paula. 'Sarah, she had no problems, I mean . . .'

Paula shook her head. 'I don't know. She was doing well at school, seemed to have plenty of friends. The usual worries, I suppose, but nothing . . . She didn't get on with her father.' The words came out almost unbidden and immediately she felt she had uttered a betrayal. 'I mean, a lot of teenagers have problems with their parents, there was nothing. I didn't mean . . . Oh God, I'm making this sound much worse than it is. He's gone out tonight,' she added irrelevantly. 'These days he's always going out.'

She looked up suddenly as though a thought had struck her. 'Terry's father. He wouldn't have gone to his father? No, I suppose you already thought of that.'

Judith sat quite still, the coffee cup still clasped tightly between her hands. 'Oh no,' she said, keeping her voice as steady as she was able. 'We're divorced, you see. I mean, obviously you realized that. Terry's father walked out of our lives when Terry was just six years old. Terry wouldn't even think of going to him.'

5.30 p.m.

The search warrant had been applied for as soon as David Martin had debunked. It had been granted in a special session and served mid-afternoon. Mike's beeper went when he was halfway back to Tynan's place. He pulled over on to the grass verge and called in, then turned his car around and headed back to Norwich.

The search was well under way by the time he got there. White-clad figures, their hands covered in surgical gloves, moving from room to room giving the impression that they really knew what they were looking for.

'The lady was an actress then,' someone commented. Mike took the proffered book of clippings and reviews. There were, he saw, glancing across at the shelves, about a dozen such books.

A shout from upstairs distracted him. He went up to the second bedroom. David's room, he thought, seeing the men's clothes lying on the bed and the shaving gear on the shelf. He thought about Davy's assertion that they had been lovers, wondering how much this room had seen.

The magazines were nothing unusual, soft-porn top-shelf editions, and Mike was ready to dismiss them, but one edition was being thrust into his hands, open at the centrefold. It had been marked by a bulky envelope slipped between the pages.

'Bit of a looker, guv! Marianne,' he commented, looking at the name that headed the page.

Mike opened the envelope and tipped the contents carefully on to the bed. About a dozen photographs fell out. Polaroids of the woman in the centrefold. The poses were amateur and the photography of questionable ability, but there was no doubt but that it was the 'Marianne' of the centrefold. Blonde hair, blue eyes, her body more graceful than voluptuous. She gazed out at the photographer, her expression slightly uncertain. A quality of innocence, despite the lewdness of some of the poses, that was highly charged. Genuinely seductive, Mike caught himself thinking.

He shoved the thought to the back of his mind and took a pen from his jacket pocket. Used it to flip the photos over. With the third, he struck lucky. There was a date, some eighteen months previous, and a name.

'Marion,' Mike said softly.

Chapter Twenty-Two

6 p.m.

Price and Morrow had retreated to the Red Lion in Avebury. It was still early enough for the dining-room to be relatively empty and they found a table at the back of the room where they could talk about the case in relative privacy.

'Nice this,' Price commented, looking around the comfortably furnished dining-room with its heavy beams and warm lighting. The food was good too, he thought, realizing just how hungry he was and how long the day had been.

Outside, although it was only six o'clock, the night was closing in, fended off slightly in the pub yard by the only street-light in the entire village.

Morrow was eating with great enthusiasm and didn't seem to want to be interrupted. Price got on with his own meal in equal silence. He was beginning to like Morrow. The man was blunt to the point of rudeness, drove like a maniac and seemed terminally prone to bossiness. But he had an energy and drive that Price guessed he was going to enjoy, and a commitment to the job that matched Price's own.

Morrow's large hand reached into his pocket, withdrew a small carton of single cream, opened it and dumped it in his coffee. He'd pocketed about a dozen of these little cartons when they'd been ordering their meal, and about the same amount of sugar, brown and white in little packets.

Price waited for the sugar to emerge from the big man's pocket. He was disappointed. Morrow drank it without.

'Tell me something,' he said. 'All that stuff you half-inched. You a klepto or what?'

Morrow slurped his coffee noisily. 'Probably,' he said. 'But I'm getting help.'

'Oh?'

Morrow nodded solemnly. 'I'm training my sergeant,' he said. 'So far she's only got the hang of sugar. Women have stupid pockets, have you noticed that? No room for anything but a lipstick and a pack of tissues. I mean, what the hell use is that?'

Price shook his head. 'Yeah, but they have handbags,' he pointed out.

'Not our Beth. Doesn't believe in them.'

He wolfed a few more mouthfuls of steak pie, sucking up more coffee without first swallowing the mouthful of food.

Price shuddered inwardly and looked away, half-nauseated, half-amused.

Morrow swallowed again, then said, 'She died of smoke inhalation but there was enough of a cocktail of drugs and drink in her system that I doubt she knew much about it.' He paused, prodded at his pie once more. 'Bloody hope she didn't know anyway. Hell of a mess.'

'There was enough soft tissue left for the tox results and blood typing then?' Price enquired.

Morrow nodded. 'Practically pickled, she was, probably had been for days, the surgeon reckons. All body tissues saturated.'

'Well,' Price observed, 'she sure as hell didn't drive there.'

Morrow guffawed, at least that's what Price thought it was. 'The car she was found in was stolen two or three days before her death. The owner was away so there were no reports, but witness statements have given us a rough fix. It was a BMW 3 series before they killed it,' he said with feeling. 'Quality. Whether that says anything or not I couldn't tell you.'

He paused, chewed thoughtfully for a moment or two, then said almost wistfully, 'Amazing things women's bodies. I mean, if she'd been a man we'd have known a whole lot less about her.' He looked deliberately at Price, leaning forward slightly, and said, 'Did you know that the womb is often the last thing to be destroyed? Symbolic that, don't you think?'

Price laughed, he couldn't help himself, then he sobered. 'The question is,' he said, 'who killed her and what the hell does she have to do with Theo Howard?'

6 p.m.

Davy had given John no trouble. He had driven him back to Divisional HQ at Norwich and delivered him quietly to the front desk. The custody officer had taken over from there.

John, waiting for Mike to finish Davy's interview, had made a statement telling how Davy had arrived on his doorstep. Then he'd drunk several cups of tea with the desk sergeant in the tiny, untidy room behind the front office.

'You miss the job?' the desk sergeant asked him. He knew John, had been around long enough to remember him as a serving officer.

Tynan nodded. 'Old habits and all that, but I fill my time one way or another.' He smiled. 'It's hard though, wanting to get stuck in and being kept on the sidelines like some damned civilian.'

'You knew the dead woman.'

'Theo, yes, my wife and I grew up with her, well, her older sister really.' He paused, settled himself more comfortably in his chair. He had no real right to be here, aware he was trading on his past reputation and on Mike's friendship. But what the hell, it was a quiet Sunday evening and the opportunity to talk shop with old colleagues didn't come up all that often.'

'So,' he said, 'anything new on this other business . . .?'

Mike sat down at the table and started the tape, going through the usual formalities. Time of interview and those present. 'Mr Martin has not requested the services of a lawyer,' he said, 'but understands that he may do so at any time and that the interview will then terminate until such time as one can be made available.'

He looked across at David Martin. 'You have been made aware of your rights, Mr Martin?' Mike asked quietly.

'Yes, yes, thank you, yes.'

'And you understand the information that you have been given?'

'Yes, I understand,' Davy said. 'I understand it all.'

Mike tipped the envelope from the evidence bag and emptied the photographs on to the table top.

'Do you recognize these, Mr Martin? For the record, Mr Martin is being shown photographs found in his room at Miss Howard's house. They will be listed as exhibit B1.'

Davy looked at the pictures and swallowed hard. 'Yes, I recognize them,' he said. 'I took them.'

'And the woman in the picture,' Mike asked. 'Who is she?'

'A girlfriend. She was a girlfriend. Ex-girlfriend now of course.' He laughed nervously.

'Why "of course", Mr Martin?'

David Martin looked surprised. 'Well, because of Theo, of course. I never looked at another woman after Theo.'

'And your relationship with Theo Howard, for the record?' Mike asked him, slightly shifting tack.

'We, we were . . . I loved her.'

'You were lovers, Mr Martin, is that what you are telling me?'

'You know it is.'

'And this other woman, this former girlfriend.' Mike changed direction once again. 'Can you tell me her name?'

David was looking puzzled now. 'I don't see . . .' he began.

'Just answer the question, please.'

'But it's not relevant. Look, I told you, I never looked at another woman after Theo. These pictures, she asked me to take them. She meant nothing to me after Theo.'

'She must have meant something for you to have kept the photographs,' Mike said. 'Her name please, Mr Martin.'

For a moment David Martin stared at him, then he said, 'It's Marion. Marion O'Donnel. I knew her for a little while when I was living in London. She asked me to take them for her. Some magazine she wanted to get into. I don't know. She did some modelling or something for them afterwards.'

Mike took the second evidence bag from his folder and laid the magazine on the table. 'This magazine?'

Again Davy swallowed hard and nodded that it was.

'For the record,' Mike intoned, 'Mr Martin is nodding.'

'What does this have to do with Theo?' Davy was asking. 'I came here because of Theo, not because of some other woman.'

There was a knock on the interview room door, a whispered consultation between someone outside and the PC sitting in on the interview. Mike was called out. He returned moments later with a second envelope and added its contents to those already on the table.

'Did you also take these, Mr Martin?'

David stared in silence at the images strewn across the table. Pictures of Theo in various stages of undress. She had taken care of herself and her body was still well-shaped and firm. She laughed playfully into the camera as though it was all some huge joke. These pictures were not pornographic, merely intimate, and Mike felt suddenly too much like a voyeur.

'You took these also, Mr Martin?'

'Yes, I took them. Theo asked me to.'

There was a catch in the younger man's voice. Tears caught in the back of his throat. Mike pushed forward.

'And now Theo's dead,' he said softly. 'Dead, Just like Marion O'Donnel. Strange coincidence, don't you think, Mr Martin?'

Chapter Twenty-Three

8 p.m.

Max turned the pages slowly. The books were like old friends to him now. His closest confidants.

He rarely saw Jake, to speak to anyway, though he followed his career closely through the newspaper reports and the work that Jake put out. Jake always made sure Max Harriman had his copy of a new work. Jake always knew where Max could be found no matter how many times he moved.

Max could not say the same. It was years since he had known exactly where Jake made his home. He had a flat in London; Max had borrowed it a time or two, he had a key. Marion had used it too when she worked there, and, Max knew, others went in and out, using the place as a letter drop and collection point. But that was not where Jake lived. As far as Max knew, it was not even a place where Jake spent the night.

He missed Jake, missed the closeness of their early years when he and Jake and the rest had been the best of friends. He often thought about them, the kids he'd gone to school with. Had them in his cuttings books too, when they'd done anything worth recording.

One was inside. Armed robbery, three counts. Others had gone their own, more respectable way. He had the notices of marriages and births and even deaths of half a dozen others he and Jake had known. But it was only

Jake that had made it to the big time. Jake who'd seen the greater picture, known that nothing really mattered so long as you were following your own particular star.

He turned the pages, pausing at one particular entry. Jake's first really successful film. It was the story of a police raid on a sex shop and the seizure of some special stock that Jake had provided for them.

It had been tame beside the stuff he was producing now, Max thought, but he still had his copy, he hung on to it knowing it would be worth an absolute packet some day.

Jake stared out into the garden through his conservatory window. He had a night sight in his hand and had spread food on to the lawn hoping they would come back. The badgers had made his garden a regular stopping-off point and Jake had come to like watching them. They were a family group, both parents and three little cubs. He liked to watch as they came snuffling through the long grass near the hedge and nosing around at the scraps he put down for them. They argued over the food like nursery school kids at a Christmas party.

Jake liked the creatures far more than he liked the average human.

He scowled suddenly, remembering Marion, how close she could get to them before they ran away.

It soothed him a little, remembering that, though his pride still hurt at just how much he had misjudged her. But he knew he must let the anger go now. If things as wild and fey as the badgers could be taken in by that stupid, nosy cow, then it was not so bad that Jake could make that same mistake too.

It would be the last time, though, Jake made that promise to himself. The very last.

8.30 p.m.

Sitting in the Myers' house had brought back so many memories for Judith. It was, in many ways, so like the house her grandparents had owned. Tall and imposing, in truth a little in need of modernization and repair, but a place Judith had loved.

She remembered the big kitchen, the two halves of it, divided for the preparation of milk and meat. The long wooden table. The family gathered, generations of it, at Sabbath, at festivals.

Judith's father had married outside his faith and Judith had been their only child. It had been hard on her grandparents, she knew, but they had accepted it. Her parents had divorced when she was three and Judith spent holidays with her father. Mostly with her grandparents.

With her mother, she lived one life. At her grandparents' house she lived another, one steeped in ritual and tradition. In music and stories. Sometimes, she thought, the stories had seemed far more real than the everyday world of school and her mother's home. She had loved the stories, told in her grandfather's sonorous voice. Elaborate tales to be narrated slowly, savoured like a fine wine.

Judith winced at the analogy. The strongest thing she allowed herself these days was coffee and it would stay that way. For Terry's sake.

She remembered that day clearly, so clearly. That final Pesach she had spent with them. Terry had been five years old, the youngest child present. Her grandfather the patriarch, in his dark suit, sitting at the head of the table. Judith herself heavily pregnant with her second child and deeply, deeply unhappy with the way her world was turning.

Terry, the youngest child, a little shy because it was the first time he had played the role, going to her grandfather and asking the question. Asking why they were celebrating with the bitter herbs and the salt and the Passover Lamb. His great-grandfather sitting him on his knee and telling the story of the flight from Egypt and the days his people had spent in the wilderness before they came finally to the promised land.

'Were you there?' Terry had asked him, his eyes round and innocent.

'No, I'm not quite that old, my boy.'

And then the final words, the pledge to celebrate the festival next year in Jerusalem. Next year. And Judith could remember her feelings of utter and complete despair. Remember also how much she had craved a drink, the partial oblivion that alcohol would provide.

Next year in Jerusalem. She'd heard that every bloody year since she could remember and that next year had never, ever come. Not for her grandparents, not for her father, not for her.

Her grandfather had told her once that Jerusalem

represented a dream. The image of fulfilment and the precious treasure of the soul.

She could remember his face when he had said those words. The conviction in his eyes.

'You'll find your Jerusalem,' he'd told her. 'You will see.'

But Judith knew that, search as she might, she never would, unless she glimpsed it briefly in the bottom of a glass.

She remembered how she had excused herself then. Got awkwardly to her feet with the weight of the second child wanting to drag her down. Had hurried from the room and sneaked into the kitchen. A half-empty bottle of whisky lay hidden at the bottom of her bag. She took a teacup from the cabinet and poured herself a large measure, drinking it down almost without tasting.

Then another.

Judith could taste it now, sitting in her tiny kitchen, hugging a cup of cooling coffee between her hands. Disgusted with the memory of herself, craving oblivion in spite of her disgust. Looking out of the window at the pouring rain, she thought of her son. Of what had happened with Terry.

8.30 p.m.

Davy lay on his back on the bench in the police cell and thought of Theo.

He had touched her when he'd found her dead. He'd

told no one that. Touched her face, her hair, the curve of her breast and hip, imagining the flesh beneath.

He had felt no disgust at her death, at the smell of sick and alcohol, only a strange sense of detachment that this woman, lying so still on the couch, was the same woman that had shared his bed. Finally, Davy had taken a comb from his pocket and combed out Theo's hair, arranging it across the pillow. He had still been holding the comb in his hand when the banging on the front door had broken the spell. Then the police had been there and life had become so much more complicated.

He fell asleep and dreamed of Theo. Theo lying beside him, her body still warm and the grey hair tangled about her face. She reached out, wrapping him in her arms, drawing him close, her body curving against his. And he, responding so strongly to her touch that even in his sleep he felt himself grow hard. Wanted her. Breathing in time to her rhythm, breathing her breath as if they were a single being.

Then Theo dissolving, becoming another woman with fairer hair and lips stained so red they seemed to drip with blood. The woman pressing her mouth against his, sucking the air from him as he wrapped her tight, pinning her to the ground.

He felt her body writhing beneath his own. The arousal and the fear blending into a single emotion as he held the woman hard enough to cause her pain, pulling away from her kisses that were not kisses and threatened to suck the breath from his lungs.

In his sleep, Davy cried out, struggling to control her. He'd never felt so much strength in anyone, man or woman, as he felt now. She had one hand free and he fought to catch her wrist again, throwing his whole weight down on top of her.

With a cry of pain, Davy woke, just as the woman's red tipped hands flashed out to rake across his face.

11.15 p.m.

It had taken only a hour or two to find her, but then he knew the places to look now. Had watched her enter the pub with her friends, followed them inside, sat drinking only feet away from them all evening without them paying any notice. The pub crowded enough for a lone drinker not to draw too much attention, and anyway, he'd gone through the pretence of waiting. Looking at his watch, showing reluctance when someone wanted to use the chair next to his. He'd been too clever to be noticed, he was sure of it.

He had left just before the group had broken up, the first couple going off just about the time he did, turning towards the main road, too preoccupied to pay him any mind.

He'd made certain that the girl had been alone. No boyfriend, one of four in the group who'd obviously been singles.

Then he'd waited, parked in a side street with a view of the main door. She could have left the other way, of course. And if she had, slipping out of the side door, then that would have been it. But he was certain she would not.

His waiting time paid off. She came out of the main door with two other friends. He waited some more, breathing shallow with anticipation as they stood a minute or two and talked on the pub step. Then the couple turned one way and the girl the other.

Yes! Yes!

He followed slowly, waiting until she had walked almost out of sight before starting the car. Would she go left towards the bus station or turn right down the side road towards the park?

Right towards the park.

Right towards the park.

He drew the car into a side street and got out quickly. His feet in their soft-soled shoes made little noise on the pavement. He followed, keeping the same distance behind her all the way until she reached the spot he wanted, where the road swung left and there was a small patch of derelict ground.

Then he ran, grabbing her from behind and using his momentum to take her down.

This one wasn't like the last. She didn't fight. Just lay there, stunned, her mouth opened in a silent scream, her breath stinking of alcohol and cigarettes.

The smell nauseated him so he hit her anyway, striking again and again at the side of her head until it lolled back at an awkward angle, blood staining the lips an even deeper red.

Monday,
19 December

Chapter Twenty-Four

3 a.m.

Terry woke up cold and stiff, realizing that the fire had burned itself out.

He swore under his breath and eased his arm from around Sarah's shoulders, feeling the familiar pins and needles sensation in his fingers. He'd been in one position far too long.

Sarah opened her eyes with a start. 'What's going on? Oh, it's freezing.'

'The fire's gone out.'

He tried to get it started again while Sarah scraped around for more kindling and fuel.

'What time will it get light?' she asked him.

'I don't know. It's getting light when I get up usually, so I suppose about seven.'

'Right.' She fell silent, hugging herself against the cold and staring into the fire as though willing it to burn. She didn't need to voice what they both were thinking. That was hours away, and it looked as though it was still going to be raining. Then, even when they got to Oaklands, there was no guarantee that the woman Terry wanted to see would be there. She hadn't been there yesterday morning and they hadn't dared to go back again twice in one day. Would she be back today? Sarah didn't feel she could spend much longer cooped up in this freezing cold semi-derelict house. She was hungry and tired and fed up with being damp and cold.

With an effort, she tried to put her doubts aside.

'My gran had a real fire,' she said. 'In her old house, before she moved to the bungalow. We used to make toast on it sometimes, in the winter.'

'Wish we had some bread, we could give it a try. I'm starved.'

'Yeah.'

'There's that little village not far up the road. The shops'll be open soon.'

Sarah sighed heavily. It all seemed so unreal; home seemed so far away.

'We've got to call home,' she said. 'They'll be worried sick.'

'I know.'

They fell silent again, guilt creeping in and preventing words. Then Sarah asked him, 'Why did you run away? I mean really.'

He didn't look as though he was ready to answer. She pushed harder.

'Look, Terry, I've stuck by you all through this, I'm not going to run out on you now.' She paused, listening to the rain outside, waiting. 'I think I deserve to know, don't you?'

Terry shook his head. 'You wouldn't understand,' he said.

'Try me! God's sake, Terry, I think you owe me that much.' She paused, reached out and took his hand. 'Please.'

He looked sideways at her, then moved closer, sitting

side by side, staring into the fire as he began. He really liked Sarah, a lot. Wanted her to be his proper girlfriend, and he knew he could only do that if he was honest with her.

But still, it was so hard. The habit of silence so ingrained that it was near impossible to break. Doctor Lucas had been easy to talk to. She'd made it clear from the start that she was used to hearing stuff, all kinds of stuff that might shock other people. And she had never shown anything either in her face or in the tone of her voice that had made him feel that she was judging him, hating him the way he knew so many people would.

He took a deep breath. 'I had a baby brother,' he said. 'He died when he was only two weeks old.'

He pulled away from her, turned so that he could see the expression on her face. 'They said I killed him, Sarah.'

Chapter Twenty-Five

7.45 a.m.

Price woke up in a strange bed, his usual early morning confusion mitigated by the untuneful shouts coming from the bathroom next door.

For a moment Price thought that Morrow was in pain, then he realized that he was singing in the shower. Splashing energetically and bellowing something unidentifiable at the top of his voice.

Price groaned, dragged himself out of bed, pulled his dressing-gown on and went in search of a cup of coffee. The clock said a quarter to eight but it felt like only five minutes since he had dragged some sheets on to Charlie Morrow's spare bed and just managed to collapse into it before falling asleep.

He found the kitchen on the second try. The first door had revealed a through lounge with a dining-table at one end and a three-seater sofa with matching chair at the other. There wasn't a great deal in between and what there was was veiled in a layer of long undisturbed dust. There was one clean area in the room, which told him a lot more about Charlie Morrow. The alcove next to the fireplace and opposite the solitary armchair was occupied by some remarkable looking hi-fi, stacked on several levels of custom-built racking. And it was clean, spotlessly clean.

Price found the kitchen at the next try and was

relieved that, if not up to the pristine standards of the hi-fi, it was at least less dirt-ridden than the rest of the living-room. There were cups in the drainer and a kettle on the side with a tea caddy and a large blue jar marked 'Coffee'. The morning, thought Price, was looking up.

Somehow, he wasn't surprised to find the sugar bowl crammed with little packs of sugar, or the fridge piled up with tiny cartons of half cream and UHT milk.

Curious, he opened a cupboard door. Plastic packs of ketchup and mayonnaise, tartare sauce and French mustard showered down on him.

'Shit!' Price muttered, picking stuff up and pushing it safely back behind the cupboard door just as the man himself walked in.

'Find everything?' Morrow said, grinning broadly.

'Is there anything you don't pinch?' Price asked him irritably.

Morrow's smile broadened. 'Believe me, Sergeant, my criminal tendencies are very specialized. Sleep well?'

'Not bad.'

'Right, how about breakfast?'

Price eyed him cautiously. 'You mean you actually have *food* in this kitchen?'

Morrow looked offended. 'Don't be silly,' he said. 'We'll head over to Mickey's place. What I've got in store for you this morning, Sergeant, you'll need a good breakfast inside you.'

Price took his coffee and went off to get dressed. He wasn't quite sure he wanted to know what Charlie Morrow had planned.

7.45 a.m.

Max was watching the video again. The one he'd first seen all those months ago.

'Marianne', as she was billed simply in the credits, had been the most beautiful thing he'd laid eyes on. That thick golden hair and pale skin and the way she'd reddened her mouth so much her lips seemed coated with fresh blood.

She was dressed in black. A tight gown that clung to every curve. The two men with her, undressing her, seemed to peel the dress from her body as though she was shedding a second skin. He watched as she lifted her arms above her head, turning towards the camera, rejoicing in the way the camera adored her body.

He imagined he held the camera in his hands now, reviewing every frame as though through an imaginary lens. Panning shots, close-ups, focusing on his favourite poses as Marion moved across the room, the two men with her caressing her body, stroking down the length of it, guiding her towards the king-sized bed.

Then, abruptly, he switched off the video. He was growing bored with these pictures of Marion, tired of the same old image.

He picked up the remote and flicked through the channels, trying to find some local news. Would they have found the body yet? Not likely, he supposed, that would be to expect efficiency from the police and he'd seen no evidence of that so far.

He switched back to the video, letting the film run while he showered and dressed. He liked this, playing after-dark film like this in broad daylight, even if he did still have his curtains closed. Enjoyed the secrecy of it. That feeling that he could go where others would not go. Do what others dare not do. Think about his next move in his game even while he went about the day-to-day, the ordinary. The mundane.

7.50 a.m.

Mike had spent the night at Maria's. He was woken by the insistent ringing of the telephone; the collator back at divisional HQ was phoning to tell him that yet another force had called in about the sex attacker and possible links.

Mike listened. 'Manchester area, about five years ago. They're faxing the stuff down to us.'

'Right,' Mike said. Then after a pause he voiced what had been on his mind for some time now. 'Why hasn't this been cross-referenced before?'

'We did make a start after the third attack,' he was told, 'but Superintendent Flint was convinced this was a localized event. Didn't want to start a panic. Anyway, this new stuff's five years old. You know how it is, takes a lot to jog memories when you've already got a backed-up case load. If a perp goes quiet for a while we all breathe a sigh of relief and don't ask too many whys. It's only when stuff gets national coverage like this that the little grey cells start nagging. Looks as though our man has history anyway.'

Mike thanked him and was about to ring off when

a thought struck him. It was pure impulse, but he said, 'Pull anything we've got on Phillip Myers, will you, Bill. It's probably nothing, but his alibi for the last attack was what you might call flimsy. He claims he was just driving around after another row with the wife. He says that she was the one who scratched his face as well. But you never know. And run a previous address check on both him and David Martin going back the last five years. Get someone to track down their work records too, see if either had a job that let them be where we need them to be at the relevant time.'

'OK. Will do. Anything else?'

Mike asked briefly about David Martin and was told that he was on the roster for the duty solicitor to see him first thing. Mike had left him in the cells to think things over for the night, but knew that he either had to charge him with something definite soon or let him go. Frankly, he didn't think he had a hope in hell of getting anything to stick as far as Theo's death was concerned. The timing was all wrong. David Martin had been at work until a half-hour before discovering Theo's body, and it would have taken close on that time to get home even at the tail end of the rush-hour. So unless he had slipped away from work, committed the crime and then gone back and finished his afternoon, Mike had to admit that he was off the hook.

He'd held him overnight, questioned him until late, then left the statement-taking to the night shift. His alibis for the nights the women had been attacked had been shaky, but, Mike had to admit, if he'd been asked to account for his actions on five separate occasions over a twelve-month period he'd have needed help piecing it together.

David Martin had been willing to have a blood sample taken and that could be compared to what they already had. And they could run a match on the DNA, though that would take time. It could be said that his willingness to give blood was a point in David Martin's favour, but he wouldn't be the first criminal to think himself too clever for the police no matter how much help he gave them. In the meantime, all Mike could do was accept that Martin would be released that morning and have him watched.

If Flint would assign him the manpower.

If David Martin didn't skip out on them before that could be arranged.

Irritated, he shook his head, wondering if he was barking up the wrong tree anyway.

'Penny for them,' Maria said.

'Not worth that much.' The phone was by the bed and she was still stretched out beside him. For a moment he was tempted to say sod the day and stay with her. Forget the problems and the responsibilities for a little while. Then he sighed, swung his legs out of bed.

'Got to go.'

'You're headed for London?'

'That's right. Magazine publishers. I'm having a last word with David Martin first, in case he's thought of anything else, then to the publishers. See if they featured Marion O'Donnel in anything else. And, for that matter, if David Martin sold them anything else.'

'He says not, presumably?'

Mike nodded. 'According to him, he took the pictures, kept some she didn't want as souvenirs and off she went. He claims that was more than a year ago, before he even knew Theo Howard.'

'Do you believe him?' Maria asked.

Mike hesitated for a moment, then nodded. 'As a matter of fact I do,' he said. 'I also believe, for what it's worth, that he loved Theo. And I'm being forced to the conclusion that he probably didn't kill her.'

'You've got something for me?' Mike said as he arrived at the police station.

The collator nodded. 'It's about our other runaway and his mother. The Ryans,' he said. 'Took a bit of rooting, I'm afraid, but this is what I've come up with.' He handed the printouts to Mike, who leant comfortably against the wall and began to read.

'As you'll see, Mrs Ryan was arrested almost three years back for being drunk in charge. In fact she's only just got her licence back. She had a drink problem but she'd been on the wagon for a good eighteen months, only fell off again when she was refused custody of her son, Terry. He'd been living with his grandparents, been in care before that, going back to when he was six years old.'

Glancing through the printout, Mike could visualize the circuitous route the collator must have taken to put all this together. Communication between different departments was not what you might call good at the best of times.

'The grandparents didn't oppose their daughter's claim on her son but the courts did, the first time she applied, anyway. It must have been one hell of a disappointment. She was absolutely soused when they picked her up. Amazing she was still conscious, never mind able to get the key in the ignition and the car started.'

'What about the father?' Mike scanned but found no trace of him. 'She said he'd left them when Terry was about six . . . What's this?'

'I thought you'd be impressed. The inquest ruled an open verdict on the child's death. There was just the possibility that the padding round the cot wasn't tied properly and simply fell down, but there were doubts. I've included the summary. You want the court records it'll have to be tomorrow morning.'

Mike nodded. 'There was talk that Terry did it,' he said.

The collator shrugged. 'The kid was six. Just six, it was his birthday. And if the mother was drunk then, who the hell knows what went on? Still, makes you think, don't it?'

Mike nodded. 'Thanks. And let me know if you find out anything about Myers,' he said.

He closed the file. The teenager seen running away from the murder scene. Was that Terry?

Mike arrived at Judith's flat just as the rain had begun to fall again. He parked the car and ran inside, closing the door on the downpour. Judith was in. She came to the flat door with a half-anxious, half-expectant look on her pale face. Mike introduced himself.

'Oh,' she said. 'You're that other one's boss. Does this mean you've heard from Terry?'

'No, I'm sorry. May I come in?'

She stood aside, directing him through into the living-room with a gesture of her hand.

'Please sit down. Can I make you any coffee? Tea?'

Mike shook his head. 'Terry hasn't called?'

'No . . .' The question hung in the air. 'Have Sarah's parents . . .?'

'She called them, yes, I heard just before I came over. She didn't say much, apparently, just that she was sorry and that she had something important to do. They think it was something to do with Terry.'

'With Terry? What could Terry possibly have to do?'

'A bus driver thinks he saw Sarah, and that Terry was with her,' Mike said. 'Saturday night about ten o'clock. He's sure he dropped them off just outside Hoton. Can you think of any reason he might be going there?'

Judith shook her head. 'Hoton?' she said. 'I'm not even certain where that is.' She hesitated. 'Isn't Oaklands out that way?'

'Oaklands?' Mike questioned.

Judith nodded slowly. 'Terry's had a few problems. He goes out there to see a counsellor. A woman called Dr Lucas.' She hesitated, then went on. 'He's a good boy,' she said. 'I don't know why they think he needs to see her. He's fine, no problems now. Just gets on with his life.'

She met his eyes deliberately, her expression implying that she thought that Mike should let him do the same. Mike's brain was working overtime. Terry went out to see Maria?

'Would you like to talk about it, Mrs Ryan? If I understood why Terry needed therapy, I might have more idea of why he ran away.'

Judith shook her head. 'It's nothing to do with him running away,' she said. 'Nothing at all.'

'If Terry had problems . . .' Mike began again, but Judith was on her feet now, clearly ready for him to go.

'Look,' she said. 'He did have some problems, but we've sorted them out and he's just fine now. Ask that psychiatrist woman, she'll tell you just the same. Terry deserves to be left alone. Allowed to get on with his life and not be hassled by every official Tom, Dick or Harry who has nothing better to do. Now. You've told me all there is to tell me and I'd rather you went.'

Mike rose to go. 'If that's the way you want it, Mrs Ryan,' he said, surprised at the anger he seemed to have provoked. 'We've only Terry's interests at heart though. All of us.'

Judith said nothing, she had turned away from him, blanked him out as though he was no longer there.

'I'll let you know if I hear anything,' Mike said quietly and left.

Maria had just reached Oaklands when Mike got through to her on his mobile and told her what Judith Ryan had said.

'Actually,' he said, 'she told me that Terry was fine, didn't need the likes of you and me nosing around and practically threw me out on my ear.'

'Wise woman. Bloody policemen.'

Mike could hear the smile in her voice as she said it, imagine the dark eyes laughing. He sighed.

'Have you spoken with Judith Ryan? I assume you have.'

'Once. At Terry's initial assessment. Terry's not one of my usuals, you know.'

'Really.' Mike thought of the mix of schizophrenics and bipolar depressives that made up the bulk of Maria's case load. Oaklands had three in-patient wards and a small secure unit. But these were separate from the old building in which Maria lived and which housed offices and out-patient clinics as well as flats for the on-site staff and rooms for those on call.

Maria rarely dealt with juveniles.

'So, how did you come by Terry?'

'He's just turned sixteen; in legal terms he's not yet adult, but in terms of funding he's come to the end of the line as a juvenile. It took a bit of fiddling, but his social worker, Mina Williams, she was convinced Terry would benefit from further intervention. The kid had just come to live with his mother, and the pair of them were doing their best to come to terms with all the changes. To abandon him, take away all support systems now seemed, well, stupid.'

'But I thought you said all funding had dried up.'

Again, he could hear the smile in her voice. 'I had a

free hour or so. Enough private patients in between the national health ones to pay for the car, so . . .'

'So Terry's a charity case?'

'The Americans would call it Pro Bono. I think that sounds so much nicer.'

'I see.' He laughed. 'But I suppose the confidentiality clause still stands whether you're getting paid or not.'

'Got it in one. Look, talk to his social worker, she'll be able to point you in the right direction at least.'

Mike had to leave it at that. Clearly, he wasn't going to get any co-operation from Judith and Maria couldn't help him. Mike had met Mina Williams on several occasions. She'd been present in loco parentis when he'd been interviewing juveniles. He liked her, but she was a tough lady, client's rights coming first in her book. What was she going to tell him that Maria would not? Until an hour or so ago he'd assumed he was just dealing with a sixteen-year-old Mispa. Now he thought of the boy seen running away from Theo's house and he was not so sure.

Judith stood beside the window, looking down at Mike Croft's car and willing him to drive away. The big old estate car seemed to dominate the street, to mark her house out for special attention, and she wished fervently that he would go.

She had played it all wrong. Lost it at the very moment when she should have been cool and calm, or even just upset by Terry's going. He could have accepted that, she thought. Understood it.

But she was so sick of all the prying and the fussing. Even now, when everything was going so well and she had begun to feel that she and Terry finally had the chance to lead a normal life, everything was going against them.

'Oh, Terry,' Judith whispered, suddenly angry with her son for jeopardizing it all. 'What the hell did you have to run off for?'

Chapter Twenty-Six

They had talked through the night. It had been hard, at first, seeing the shock on Sarah's face, so hard that he'd wanted to run out into the storm and get far away from her. Then the shock had faded.

'I don't believe it,' she had said. 'I don't believe they could think that about you. And besides,' she'd added as though this made it impossible, 'you were just a little kid.'

'I don't remember much,' Terry said miserably. 'If I did it, I don't remember doing it. I know I was jealous of Nathan, but I mean, lots of kids are jealous, aren't they?' He didn't look at Sarah, but felt her nod, he willed himself to carry on. 'I remember, I'd gone into Nathan's room and I shouldn't have been there. They'd given him my baby toys. Said I was too grown up for them and that I should give them to him. I didn't want to. I cried. I remember that. It was my birthday. I was six and they'd given me all this new stuff to make up for taking my baby things away. They'd had a birthday party, all the family, that sort of thing. Then, when everyone had gone away Mum and Dad had started arguing about something. They were always fighting. I sat on the stairs for a long time listening to them. Then I went into Nathan's room.'

He clammed up again. Sarah hunted around for

something that would keep the conversation going, wanting him to open up to her.

'What were you looking for,' she said, 'in Nathan's room, I mean?'

Terry hesitated. 'You'll laugh,' he said.

'No I won't.'

He glanced sideways at her, then dug a hand into his pocket, pushing through a hole he'd made in the lining. 'It was this.'

Sarah took the proffered object with something close to reverence. 'It's a mouse,' she said, then laughed. 'Where's its other ear?'

Terry shrugged. 'Lost it a long time ago,' he said. 'I don't know how come they let me keep it really. I guess in the panic no one noticed.' He hesitated, embarrassed. Sarah could see the back of his neck and his cheeks begin to redden. He said, 'When I was really little, I didn't want teddy bears or any of the usual stuff but Mouse always slept under my pillow. When they made me give it to Nathan, well I guess it must have really pissed me off.'

He fell silent then, drawing into himself as the memory played itself out. His parents' angry voices coming up the stairs and his father slamming the bedroom door. He'd hidden behind the big cupboard in Nathan's room, afraid of his mother. She had come unsteadily into the room, leaning heavily against the bedroom door, pushing herself off from the doorframe as she lurched towards the baby's cot. She'd been drinking again. Even at six years old, Terry had understood that.

Terry had pressed himself closer to the wall, peering around the corner, watching.

Nathan's cot had also been his once. It was a white, drop-sided affair trimmed with white drapes and lace-edged bumper cushions all around the sides. From his place behind the cupboard, he lost sight of his mother behind the drapes as she bent towards the cot. Then she began to scream. A piercing, tremulous sound that had Terry cowering in the corner and his father dashing from the bedroom and bursting through the door.

Nathan was dead, one of the bumper cushions from around the cot pressed across his face.

'I was six,' Terry told her. 'It had been my birthday. But it does happen, you know.' His voice rose with a nervous edge to it. 'I mean, don't you ever listen to the news? Being a kid doesn't mean you can't kill someone. Nathan's dead, Sarah. And so's Theo.'

Chapter Twenty-Seven

9.15 a.m.

Tom Andrews had received another letter and this one worried him far more than the last. Like the others it had been hand-delivered. It was printed on cheap paper and had been addressed to him directly. That last was no real surprise, Tom's byline appeared on a weekly column and regularly on articles and reports. He was well known locally. It was the content of this last letter that troubled him so deeply.

He picked up the telephone and called Divisional. Inspector Croft was not there, he was told. On impulse, he called Maria, who was getting ready for her first patient. Mike wasn't there, she said. Off to London.

Tom knew better than to ask why; it was a concession to him that she told him that much.

He tried to reach Price, then remembered that Price too had gone elsewhere, and there seemed little point attempting to reach Mike on his mobile. He could hardly turn around and come right back just because Tom Andrews would rather deal with him.

Reluctantly, Andrews called Divisional HQ again and asked to be put through to Superintendent Flint.

He was brief and to the point. 'I've received another letter,' he said. 'He claims he's killed someone. Name of Marion.'

9.20 *a.m.*

Davy breathed deep. It was raining, but the air was cold and clean, and after a night cooped up listening to the town drunks the sound of rain and traffic was the most welcome sound in the world.

Theo's house would still be cordoned off. He had the few things with him he had collected for the night he had spent in the hotel, and his bank and Visa cards.

The duty solicitor had seen him signed out then gone on to his next case. He'd been ushered out like a guest who'd overstayed his welcome and insulted his hosts.

Davy began to walk, not knowing where to go or how to get there, his mind dwelling on the facts that seemed most important to him.

Marion was dead. Theo was dead. Two women he'd been involved with, murdered within only a few days of one another.

God, if he'd been the police, he'd have been suspicious of him, Davy thought bitterly.

He quickened his pace, turning up the collar of his coat against the rain and moving with a sudden determination.

Twice in the past year he had seen Marion. Something he'd failed to tell the police and really didn't feel he wanted to tell them now. Reason told him that his disinformation would count against him should he ever be found out, but right now Davy really didn't care.

The first time he'd seen Marion had been brief. He'd called into the bookshop where she was working, just to say hello. The second time, she had called him, had insisted they meet at Avebury, well away from anyone that might see them.

They'd walked among the stones. It had been raining and the ground was soft beneath their feet and slippery with fallen leaves. Marion's mood had seemed to match the weather, dull and miserable, but she had failed to tell him what the problem was. Seemed to regret her impulse to call him and, when he really pressed, told him it was only man trouble.

At the time he'd accepted that. It was easy to accept Marion having trouble with the men in her life. Now, he wondered. Realized he was probably withholding material evidence or whatever they called it.

He should go back really. Sort it out.

Davy hesitated for a moment but couldn't face returning to the police station and the hours of questioning that would follow. Not yet.

They had had coffee, he remembered, in the barn café, and when he had paid the poem he had composed for Theo had fallen out of his wallet. Marion had picked it up, that poem that he had written especially for Theo, and she had smiled properly for the first time.

'You wrote poetry for me once,' she had said. 'That one about the fire on Kennet Hill. You know, I really liked that.' He had only realized much later that she had not given Theo's poem back.

Theo and Marion, such different women. They had known about each other. Davy was open that way, not liking secrets. The two women had even spoken once when Marion had called him about something.

Different women, but he linked them. He had known

them both and, surely, he must somehow have drawn the thread closed between them.

There was only one link he could think of. The photographs. The magazine.

He glanced around before crossing the road, wondering if he was being tailed. Then decided it didn't matter if he was. They had nothing they could charge him with and there was no way they could keep him confined. Running across the busy road, Davy hopped on to a bus, the first that came along, looking back over his shoulder as it pulled away.

9.30 a.m.

The weather seemed to have broken at last. Grey skies had lightened and there was even a suggestion of sunlight about the day. Price was not destined to see much of it.

'Arrived late last night,' Morrow said over breakfast, producing a series of faxes from his pockets. 'Thought it best you got a bit of sleep before immersing yourself in muck for the day.'

Price took the papers from him and laid them on a spare bit of table.

Mickey's Café was Morrow's regular watering-hole. It fell somewhere between an old-fashioned transport café and a continental bar. Formica-topped tables that could have survived the fifties and old cigarette ads framed on the walls, together with a selection of film posters and painted art deco mirrors.

'This is the Howard woman,' Price commented, surprised at the poses and Theo's state of undress.

'And that's Marion O'Donnel,' Morrow confirmed. 'Interesting, don't you think?' He waved a greasy knife in Price's general direction. 'Starred in her own feature, by the look of things. July's special. So I've arranged for a root around in our "lost and found", see if the young lady was more than a one-hit wonder.'

'Marianne,' Price commented, reading the curvy lettering at the head of the page. 'You think she was a pro, then?'

Morrow took a large swallow of his tea. 'Who can say? Your boss is paying a visit to the publishers, but I thought we'd see what we've already got in stock. I've cleared it with Vice.'

Price folded the faxes and handed them back to Morrow. 'So you and I are going to spend the day looking at mucky books?'

'And the odd video.' Morrow grinned. 'Anyway, it won't be just the two of us. I've got a couple of assistants lined up.'

Morrow settled down to finishing his breakfast. Two little helpers, he thought happily. Beth Cooper was a trooper, she'd not turn a hair at anything she saw, but he was looking forward to seeing just how red Stein could get during the course of the day.

10 a.m.

Beth Cooper did a lot to improve Price's day. He put her in her middle twenties. Five five, somewhere about a hundred and twenty pounds and none of them wasted. Blonde curls, cut a bit too short for his liking – but then, she hadn't asked his opinion. Blue-grey eyes.

The young man who crept in with her was another matter. He was still a probationer, Morrow told Price. Seconded from uniform because Morrow needed bodies. 'He's all they could spare me,' Morrow had complained.

He sidled into the room, sandy-haired and pale-faced, looking far too uncertain even for a probationer, Price thought. But he remembered his own time as a police rookie far too well to pass judgement, yet. And the thought of a probationary year under a Charlie Morrow was enough to make anyone a little green about the gills.

It was funny, Price thought, after the first ten minutes of flicking through skin mags, just how boring it got, how unsexy. The women in the pictures ceased to be women, just images to compare with the pictures he had of Theo and Marion. He'd thought it unlikely that Theo would be featured in any of them. After all, she might be in good shape, but she wasn't exactly a spring chicken. He'd mentioned the thought to Morrow.

'You ever work Vice?' Morrow had asked him.

'Only briefly and it was drugs rather than porn.'

'Right. Well, I have, sonny boy, and I'll tell you for nothing. I've seen skin flicks and magazines featuring anything with a body from six months to Methuselah.'

Price tried hard to concentrate, realizing that images

were just skipping by. From across the room he heard Beth Cooper laugh. Now if he was looking at her . . .

He put the thought aside. Jesus Christ, and he didn't think these things affected him . . . He shifted uncomfortably in his seat, trying not to think of Beth Cooper and convinced of Morrow's piercing gaze upon him.

'I see brush salesmen are still in vogue,' Beth commented. 'God, Charlie, you should take a read of some of this stuff.'

Price found himself skimming through the pages of text. Sure, he'd read these things when he was younger. Not quite behind the bike sheds, but the equivalent. He was surprised to see how little they had changed.

He'd had a friend at college who had supplemented his grant writing this stuff. He'd fallen lucky and placed quite a bit with one magazine or another. Price vividly recalled one of the rejections he had got too: 'Sorry, but we're steering clear of the pseudo-lesbian stuff this month.'

It had paid better anyway than working in the student bar.

Sighing, he realized that the last few pages had just passed him by. Either woman could have been there, everything exposed, and he would not have seen them.

He went back for a second look.

'See something you like?' Charlie Morrow bellowed at him. Price's thoughts drifted to Beth Cooper sitting across the room. 'Oh yes, guv, plenty,' he said.

10 a.m.

The collator could not get hold of Mike. He knew that Mike generally dumped his mobile, switched off, in the glove compartment when he was driving and it was no use trying to get him that way. He paged him anyway and then went straight to Flint with the information.

Phillip Myers had a record. An old one, for sure, but still a record.

Flint read it through. 'Two counts of possession,' he said, 'and one count of indecency.' Satisfaction was written large on Flint's face.

'Bring him in,' he said.

Chapter Twenty-Eight

12.20 p.m.

Terry and Sarah had finally fallen asleep and it had been late morning before they woke up. The rain had eased to a light drizzle, but the skies were still leaden and threatened more. At first they had tried to keep off the roads and walk parallel to them across the fields, but with the weight of mud dragging on their feet this had proved too much. And hedges crossing the path made the trek impossible.

There was little traffic. They decided they would risk walking on the road and hope that no one took an interest.

Sarah had taken hold of Terry's hand as they left the house, surprising him. Most of the night had been spent talking and, despite the rain, Terry felt more hopeful than he could remember in a long, long time. Up until now, the only people that knew his story had been his great-grandparents and his mother and the various social workers and other professionals that had seemed to dog their lives.

The village Terry had spoken of was just ahead of them. 'Look,' he said, 'it might be better if we don't both go inside the shop just in case the police have put out a report or something. You wait round the corner. There's a bus shelter, I think, and I'll go inside.'

Reluctantly, Sarah agreed, delving in her pocket for

some of the damp money she had obtained with her mother's card. 'I think you watch too many spy films,' she said. 'They won't be interested in looking for us. Too many crimes to solve.'

'Please, Sarah,' he said.

She bit her lip. 'OK, I'll wait round the corner, but don't you think of running out on me or anything.'

'Don't be stupid.'

He left her at the bus-stop and crossed the road, disappearing inside the shop. Anxiously, Sarah watched.

He took so long that Sarah was beginning to think he really had run into trouble. Then he came out, carrier bag in hand. He walked slowly, with exaggerated casualness, until he reached the bend, then he ran.

'Come on,' he hissed at her. 'We're in the papers, both of us.'

1.45 p.m.

The main gate at Oaklands stood open and they walked through unchallenged.

'I thought there'd be security,' Sarah commented.

'Not on this part. The hospital bit, where the in-patients are, that's across the other side and I think it's got its own gate.'

They walked on up the drive, Sarah looking around with interest. 'A lake,' she said, pointing.

'Yeah, there's acres of parkland and woods and stuff, even deer. Can you imagine owning a place like this?'

Sarah grinned at him. 'Fancy cutting the grass?'

Terry was straining to see up ahead, then, suddenly, he was smiling. 'She's here,' he told Sarah. 'I can see her car.'

'Well, come on then!' Grabbing Terry's hand, Sarah began to run.

'It's all right, Pete, I know them,' Maria said.

The caretaker looked unsure, but nodded. 'OK, if you're sure.'

Terry looked gratefully at the tall black figure standing at the top of the long oak staircase. Beside him, Sarah drew a quick startled breath. However she had pictured Dr Maria Lucas, it was not as someone who could have made it as a supermodel.

She clasped Terry's hand more tightly and walked up the stairs. Maria smiled, then opened the door to her flat and ushered them inside.

'Coats off,' she said. 'You look soaked through. Get yourselves in front of the fire and I'll make some coffee, or would you like tea or chocolate?'

'Er, anything, anything would be just great,' Terry was saying.

'And Sarah?'

Sarah nodded. 'Oh, sorry. Chocolate please.'

'How do you know Sarah's name?' Terry asked suddenly.

Maria shook her head. 'You don't want publicity then remember to put a little X in the box.' She picked up a copy of the *Chronicle* and tossed it over to him. 'Now, get warm and read about yourselves.'

She went through to the kitchen and they could hear the kettle being filled and the rattle of pots. Terry seemed to have frozen to the spot, staring at the newspaper, the real shock sinking in for the first time.

Sarah took it from him and pulled him over to the fire. 'God's sake, Terry, what's the matter with you? You think people don't read the papers or something? You saw it back in that village. You knew what it said.'

He looked really scared, she thought. She was just relieved that they had made it here. But neither of them, Sarah realized, had given much thought to what they should do afterwards, or even what Maria Lucas would say to them.

She sank down on the small sofa beside Terry, laying her head against his shoulder. At first he sat stiffly, then he unbent a little and put his arm around her.

Maria came back into the room and sat down opposite them. 'The kettle will soon boil,' she said. 'Then we can talk and you can tell me what you came all this way for.'

She raised an elegant eyebrow in Terry's direction but the boy said nothing. Instead, he sat staring at the carpet as though its pattern fascinated him.

'Terry!' Sarah nudged him, then when it was clear she'd get no answer, she turned to Maria. 'Terry said you could help him.'

She nudged him again, uncertain of how much to say, then, hesitantly, 'It's about that woman, the one that died, you see. Terry thinks they're going to blame him for it.'

She stopped there, not knowing what else to say without at least Terry's tacit approval.

Maria nodded slowly, careful not to let anything of what she was thinking show on her face. So that was why he had run. He knew Theo Howard. Of course, the 'old woman' he had helped with her shopping, and Theo was an actress. Stupid not to have connected them before. And with what Terry had been accused of in the past . . . She remembered the teenager Mike said had been reported running away. 'I thought you'd come here, Terry. I rather hoped you would,' she said quietly.

'Oh?' Sarah questioned.

'You were seen,' Maria told them. 'Getting off a bus at Hoton late Saturday night. Hoton isn't far away. I thought you might be coming here.'

The boy looked up, briefly meeting Maria's eyes.

'Don't know why I did,' he said. 'Nothing you can do.'

'Are you sure of that?'

'Terry!' Sarah said again, nudging him harder this time. 'You've got to tell her.'

Maria smiled at the girl then got up and went back through to the kitchen. 'I'll get those drinks,' she said. As she disappeared through the kitchen door she could hear Sarah haranguing her friend. Telling him he'd have to talk. She closed the door quietly, hoping that Sarah would have got through to him before she went back in. It would make things so much simpler if she did. She set about preparing the drinks, arranging biscuits on a plate. Trying to give Sarah time to work on Terry.

There was a telephone in the kitchen and for a

moment she thought of calling Mike, at least to tell him that the kids were safe. She was reaching for the phone when a sudden shout from the other room turned her around and had her heading for the door.

'You've got to talk to her,' Sarah had been saying. 'You can't just sit there, Terry. You just can't.'

'How did she know about the bus?' he said.

'I don't know. Maybe it was in the paper.'

'It wasn't. I looked.'

Terry raised his head, staring into her face. She had never seen such desperation or such fear.

'Terry . . .' Sarah laid a hand on his arm.

He jumped to his feet. 'I shouldn't have got you into this. I'm sorry. What if I did do those things? If I did it to Nathan then maybe . . . What if I did it, Sarah?'

Sarah stared at him. Of course you didn't do it, she wanted to tell him. Of course you couldn't do anything like that, but the words just wouldn't come out. They seemed frozen somewhere in her throat and she couldn't get them to budge.

Just when had he started thinking like this? Had this horrific self-doubt been playing on his mind all the time that they had been together?

Suddenly, Sarah was afraid, his doubt transmitting itself to her. The fear must have shown itself on her face because Terry moved then, looking around him urgently for an escape. His gaze fell on Maria's car keys lying on the table near the door. He'd grabbed them even before Sarah realized what he was doing and was heading for the stairs. Then Sarah was on her feet as well and chasing after him, screaming out his name.

Her screams brought Maria running.

By the time Maria reached the top of the stairs Sarah was standing by the big front door. As she ran down the stairs, she heard a car engine surge into life, revving far too fast, then a sudden screech of tyres spinning on loose gravel.

She reached the door in time to see her Mazda fish-tailing wildly as Terry, not understanding power steering, swung the wheel sideways. He tried to pull it back on line again, and veered far too much the other way.

'Terry!' Maria's shout joined Sarah's screaming. 'Oh shit!'

'I tried to stop him. I tried.' Sarah was grabbing at her arm. Maria hardly heard her. She was running down the long drive after the speeding car, Sarah close upon her heels.

He'll never make that bend. Oh God, he'll never make that bend . . .

The drive swept a graceful left and then back right in another sweeping curve. Terry still didn't have the hang of the steering. She could hear from the change in engine note that he must somehow have managed to shift to second gear. 'He's not going to make the bend.'

She almost covered her eyes, but couldn't tear her gaze away as the car, in a shower of mud and gravel, veered wildly out of control and left the road heading towards the lake.

For an instant Maria stopped dead, horrified by what she saw.

'Terry!' Sarah cried again. 'Terry!'

Just for an instant, the Mazda seemed to stop dead, poised with its wheels free of the ground, a creature of the air. Then it plunged forward and dived nose-first into the lake.

Chapter Twenty-Nine

1.45 p.m.

Max Harriman was on his way to work and thinking about what Jake would be doing next.

Trying to second guess Jake Bowen was a full-time occupation and Max was pretty good at it, though he had to admit that Jake gave him a little help. Small hints here and there in the details of his attacks or the content of his films. Details that emerged from a shared past and that Max was certain few others would be able to see. Like the vicious red he drew upon his women's lips and that vampire image Jake had used now in three of his best films, mouths filled with blood sharing kisses deep enough to touch the soul.

Max smiled to himself as he remembered looking on his mother's face and that blood-red smile. Of bending over her face, his lips touching . . .

Max pulled the thoughts away. The truth was he felt restless now that he had killed the woman, eager to find another image, another story to play out.

It was lucky that Jake had come up with the last one. The Marion story had been one of the best that Max had ever told himself. Now it was time to move on, to start looking again.

1.45 p.m.

Jake was driving along the Devizes road. He was dressed in his working clothes, his jacket hanging from the loop near the back window, briefcase on the passenger seat, the very image of a perfect sales rep.

He had two more calls to make today, then he could head for home.

His road took him between the ridge of Kennet Long Barrow and the conical rise of Silbury Hill. He glanced sideways as he passed, seeing the bright orange tape of the police cordon flapping in the breeze and the dark oblong of the grass where the car had burned. It had been at the back of his mind to use the location from the moment he'd seen that poem Marion's old boyfriend had written her. It had, Jake thought, worked out well in the end.

Now Jake passed Kennet by without a second glance. He had enjoyed his time with Marion, the brief interval they had been lovers, but he had always known it couldn't last. Jake's was not a lifestyle that could easily be shared.

He shrugged lightly, his mind already turning to his next delivery. Pity she hadn't been able to keep her nose out from where it had no right to be. The day he'd found her in the second editing suite he had set up at Vinnie's place had been the day he realized their time was over. Nothing was wasted though; those final days he'd kept her in the basement had given him some useful footage and it had been good to be able to add another fire sequence to his repertoire.

Jake had been raised to let nothing go to waste.

1.45 p.m.

Mike had done his time as a probationer in King's Cross, his beat taking in the station, the seedy little hotels and the back-street strip clubs. It was a long time, though, since he'd had to drive in London, and he had forgotten just how much he hated it.

He'd managed to squeeze into a parking space, partly blocking an alleyway, beside the building that housed Primart Publications Ltd. The December day, grey and miserable, cast grimy shadows over the city street.

Mike went inside. Primart was on the second floor. He was well off his home ground here and had, as a matter of courtesy, informed his local opposite number that he'd be coming. They'd filled him in on Primart's background.

Primart Publications produced books and magazines, sex aids, videos. The usual stuff, all legal and above board. Squeaky clean, was the way it had been described to Mike, and very profitable.

They used girls from a series of agencies. Drew up official contracts with each one they used and actually went to the trouble to insist on proof of age.

'They are totally professional,' Mike's informant had told him. 'For that matter most of the bigger skin publications are. Can't afford to be otherwise. The editor was busted ten years ago for printing pictures of a fifteen-year-old girl. I saw the pictures and you'd have sworn she was five years older. They cleaned up their act after that and their processing of models. Only deal through agencies now.'

It was useful to know. If Primart was concerned with its reputation it would be more likely to co-operate.

Mike had taken the stairs. He found himself facing a pair of glass doors leading to a surprisingly plush lobby, with an elderly, blue-rinsed receptionist seated behind a solid wood desk. The lobby was decorated with potted palms and comfortable armchairs. Mike did a double-take. It looked more like the entrance to a small hotel than to a company specializing in soft porn. He found himself checking the logo on the glass doors – and his own preconceptions – before crossing to the woman at the desk and asking if the editor might be available.

He laid his identification in front of her. She took her time, putting on her glasses and reading carefully before returning it to him.

'You're a long way from home, Inspector Croft,' she said cheerfully. 'If you'd like to take a seat, I'll see if he's free. May I tell him what it's about?'

Mike reached into his overcoat pocket and produced the magazine, withdrew it from the evidence bag and laid it open at the centrefold.

'This woman,' he said. 'I need to know if she did other work for you beside this.'

'May I?' Mike nodded and she flicked back to the front, checking the date. 'Miss July this year,' she said. 'Well, it will all be on file. All our young ladies are registered, you know.'

Mike nodded. 'I'm sure.'

'She's not in any trouble, I hope?'

'If you could just tell him I'm here . . .'

'Yes, of course.' She spoke into the intercom, telling the listener that a police officer needed to speak with him. Moments later, he was being directed through to the inner office.

Darren Prestwick had been editor of the three magazines put out by Primart Publications for the previous five years. He had learnt early on that image was everything. He was a businessman and wore a business suit and an air of competence and authority that he felt went well with the job.

He listened to what Mike had to say without comment, then got up and crossed to a second desk housing a computer.

'We keep everything on a data base,' he said. 'Cross-referenced under real name and any they might have appeared under in our magazines. All of our girls come to us through an outside agent, and this one, if I'm not much mistaken, came in through Mr Vincenza.'

'Vincenza? Vinnie Vincenza, used to have a basement office, back of Holland Park?'

Darren Prestwick smiled. 'He still does,' he said. 'And a second model agency in Bristol, though he no longer runs the main business end himself. He has managers to do that.'

'Things must be looking up for him,' Mike commented.

Prestwick was manipulating the data base. 'Ah, here we are. Yes, I was right. Vincent Vincenza, came in through his London office apparently. If you give me a moment I'll print out for you. It looks as though she just did the one edition. Our monthly feature.' He frowned. 'We had her booked for a shoot last week too, but she didn't show.' He swung his chair around and gave Mike an interrogative look. 'Is there some kind of trouble, Inspector Croft? Because if there is, I'd like to know. We want our girls to have a clean background. Insist on it.'

'Did you meet Marion O'Donnel personally?' Mike asked.

'No, generally I don't. Their agents deal with ours and they do the shoot, usually in our studio out at Victoria Dock. We've got a converted warehouse down there. I approve and select the finished shots.' He paused. 'I'd like to know what your interest is, Inspector Croft.'

Mike frowned, took the magazine back and replaced it in his pocket. 'There's a good reason Marion O'Donnel didn't turn up for that second shoot,' he said. 'By that time she was dead.'

2.15 p.m.

'That was your governor,' Morrow announced as Price returned from lunch. 'He's been to see the publisher. Seems Marion O'Donnel did only the one shoot for them. Didn't live long enough to pose for any more.'

'Any mention of David Martin?'

'No. The original shots were sent in by one Vincent Vincenza. Alias Mr Brian Hammond. Offices in London, Bristol and maybe bloody Rome as well for all I know.

Your boss is planning on paying him a call this afternoon.'

'What's he driving?' Price asked automatically, thinking about Mike's wreck of a car and wondering if it would make the distance. 'No, never mind.'

Morrow gave him a puzzled look. 'He says he knows Vincenza from when he worked the King's Cross beat. He was small time then but things have been looking up for Vinnie this last year or so, bought a place out Malmesbury way. Lives there with one of his ex-models.'

'So,' Price asked, 'what's Vincenza been up to that pays so well since then?'

'That's what your boss wants to find out.'

Price glanced at the magazines stacked on his desk. 'Not much point in going through the rest of these then,' he commented.

'Not for the moment, no. Croft checked on Theo Howard, but they denied all knowledge, so, for the moment, we've drawn a blank. This afternoon though, I've got something else lined up. Took me a while to get it set up and it might not even be relevant.' He paused, frowning. 'There's just been something puzzling me ever since I saw the crime scene, the way it was laid out. Reminded me of something Vice brought in a month or two ago.'

Mike reported in, bringing Flint up to speed on his investigations.

'I think you're wasting your time looking for a link,' Flint told him. 'Martin knew the girl, just happened to give her his number. What could be more natural than that?'

'Probably nothing,' Mike agreed. 'But there's still two suspicious deaths. We have to look at all angles.'

'And one of them not even on our patch. Seems to me you're wasting resources, Croft. Anyway, we've finally got a breakthrough on our rapist.'

'Oh?'

'That's right. That file you wanted pulled on Phillip Myers? Well it panned out. He's got previous.'

'Myers has? What?'

'Conviction for indecency and a couple for possession. Agreed it's a long time ago. His student days . . .'

'And nothing since? And what exactly was the charge?'

He listened as Flint filled him in. 'It hardly adds up, sir,' he protested. 'A student prank and now a series of very violent attacks with nothing in between . . .'

'We don't know that. Myers isn't stupid. Anyway, like you said yourself, we have to check it out.'

He paused – Mike could hear voices in the background – then Flint spoke again, his voice grave. 'There's been a development. A woman's body's just been found on wasteland close to Aston Park.'

'Same MO?'

'Looks like it. I've got to go. Look, check in later with anything you turn up your end. There's something else, too. David Martin's done a bunk,' he paused. 'It was a risk we took in letting him go, but you said yourself you couldn't pin anything on him.'

'I thought you'd put a tail on him.'

'For God's sake, Mike! We don't have the manpower, you know that. Look, if we need him we'll find him and bring him in. Meantime, we've other fish to fry.'

Chapter Thirty

2.15 p.m.

Terry thought he was going to die. Then he stopped thinking, had no time for thought, as the car tore itself from his already minimal control and headed towards the lake.

He heard himself screaming, lifting his arms instinctively to protect his head. Then the stunning blow as the car hit water that felt like iron and he was thrown forward against the restraint of the seatbelt.

Winded, Terry lowered his arm and looked around in panic, blessing the ingrained habit that had made him fasten his belt. The front of the car had hit the water first and was sinking fast. In the darkness, Terry couldn't tell how far.

How deep was the water? How the hell was he going to get out?

The car had landed at a slight angle, sinking obliquely, pitching the driver's side most deeply into the water ... He dare not open the door. He tried the window, feeling along the door panel for the handle, then realized that Maria's car had electric windows. Frantically he tried to find the button, but when his fingers touched it, pressed it hard, nothing happened.

The water, he thought. It must have short-circuited. Nothing was working. He'd never get out.

He had to get into the back. Try and climb out through the back somehow.

He began to wriggle around, easing himself past the steering-wheel and into the space between the seats, grazing his leg against the gear-lever, jamming for a moment between the gear-shift and the handbrake, panicking as his clothes caught on them. He thought he'd never get himself free.

Then, he heard the hammering on top of the car.

Mike took the opportunity to try to reach Maria, hoping she had heard from Terry. He stood for a long time, listening to the phone ringing, the sound hollow in the empty flat.

He rang John Tynan and asked him to keep trying Maria, to see if there were any news of Terry.

'I was planning on going out there anyway. Maria promised me a drink after work,' John told him. 'We've got your mobile and pager numbers. I'll get back to you, soon as I can.'

'Terry? Can you hear me, Terry? Keep away from the window. Keep down.'

Her face pressed as close to the window as she could get, Maria could just make out the dark shadow of Terry's body inside the car. He seemed to be wedged between the seats. For an awful moment she wondered if he was even still conscious. Or if he had been badly injured in the crash. She tried again. 'Terry. Keep your head down and your face covered, I'm going to break the glass.'

She thought she saw him move, couldn't afford the time to be sure. Standing up to her waist in freezing water, her feet sinking into deep, foul-smelling mud and with the car sinking further at every moment, Maria knew she didn't have time for much finesse.

Were rear windows laminated, like front windscreens? She didn't know. She couldn't risk trying and then failing. The car was sinking far too fast. Hoping that Terry would have the sense to cover his face, she moved around to the side and slammed the rock she was holding with all her weight behind it into the glass.

It took three attempts before it broke. The water restricted her movements and the mud sucked at her feet, throwing her off balance, but finally she made it through. Shouting at Terry, trying to find out if he was all right, even as she used the stone to break the sharpest edges from around the window frame. The force of her blows against the glass was making the car shift, sinking even faster into the mud and slime. Finally, she was satisfied that she could get him out. She reached a hand inside. 'Terry, come on, Terry. Let me help you out.'

Almost reluctantly he unwedged himself from between the seats. His face was white. She grabbed his sweater, tugging him forward, making him turn his body so he would fit more easily through the gap she'd made. He reached forwards, trying to help himself now.

'That's it,' she encouraged. 'Keep going. That's it.'

Terry pushed against the seats with his feet. His hands reaching out, trying to get some purchase on the outside of the car. Maria pulled on any part of him she could get her hands around. Tugging at his shoulders, his sweatshirt, the belt of his jeans, until eventually he fell forward, splashing into the water on top of her, dragging them both down.

Maria struggled to stand upright, pulling the boy with her. He seemed stunned, unable to co-ordinate, and she found herself having to support him as they waded to the bank.

Sarah was there, shouting encouragement and reaching out to help them on to shore. They fell in a muddy, shivering heap, gasping for breath.

'Are you all right?' Maria demanded. Then: 'God almighty boy, no one would have blamed me if I'd let you drown! Now, come on, on your feet before we all freeze to death out here.'

By the time John Tynan arrived about half an hour later, they were back inside Oaklands. Sarah was taking her turn in the shower. Terry was wrapped in an old dressing-gown that Mike had left at Maria's place. There were cuts from the flying glass on his face and arms, but he'd been lucky; wedged between the seats, he'd been protected from the worst of it. Maria herself, muddy clothes dumped on the bathroom floor and a towelling robe wrapped around her, was trying to clear up some of the mess.

'Oh, John. Just the most welcome person. Please, make some tea or something, will you, and make sure he stays put.'

John looked at Terry, then at Maria, taking in the muddy feet emerging from beneath the towelling robe and the mess of filthy, stinking clothes she was holding in her hands.

He decided that this was not the time for questions.

From the bathroom, Sarah emerged, wrapped in Maria's dressing-gown, towelling her hair.

'Better?' Maria asked her.

The girl nodded. 'Good. You'll find the hairdrier on the shelf in the bedroom. The one next to the door. This is John Tynan, he's going to make some tea. And I'm going to get clean.'

She marched off, her pent-up anger charging the atmosphere until it almost hummed.

John surveyed them both thoughtfully. 'Terry and Sarah,' he said. 'It might be worth knowing that I've never seen her that annoyed. Just what did you two do?'

'We, Terry . . . Her car,' Sarah began. 'It's in the lake.'

John took a deep breath and exhaled slowly.

'Tea, I think,' he said. 'Strong tea.'

Chapter Thirty-One

Mike called the office again on his mobile and asked to be put through to the collator.

'Anything come through from either of the other areas?'

'I take it you've heard about Phillip Myers? Flint's been like a bloody dog with two tails since I gave him that one.'

Mike laughed humourlessly. 'I'll just bet he was. Even if Myers is our man, it still leaves another bastard on the loose, or is he planning on Myers being blood type O as well as A?'

'God knows. He'd probably give it a go. Anyway, this might interest you more. We've got two possibles so far. Neither is a perfect fit, but not bad for a beginning. One's a feller called Osbourn. Served three years of a five-year stretch for serious sexual assault. Released three years ago, faded into the woodwork since then. Originally from Manchester. He's no good for our first two victims, but those two could well be down to our other unknown. He's the right blood group for the last four and Marion O'Donnel too. We don't know about the dead woman until the path reports come in.'

'Sounds promising,' Mike said. 'And the other one?'

'The other one was sent through from Bristol. A more interesting proposition. Three charges of serious sexual assault and a series of public order offences. Seems he became obsessed by some young girl. Fits the description of our attack victims, blonde hair, blue eyes, small. She was still at school at the time, used to follow her there. Follow her home, sit outside her house until all hours. He never touched her, just made a nuisance of himself; when they finally got the evidence to pull him in on the assault charges, he disappeared. The thing was, guv, all the girls he attacked fit the same broad description. We're running it through PNC and Voters, see if he's turned up here under his own name or any of his known aliases.'

'You've informed Flint?'

'Told him we're tracking, not a lot else to tell him yet unless our man surfaces here.'

It was a long shot, Mike knew, but it sounded more likely than Phillip Myers.

'The other thing, Mike, the kids have turned up. We had a call from Oaklands. Uniform's on its way out there now.'

4 p.m.

The project Morrow had in mind was a series of videos. Morrow, Price, Beth Cooper, Stein and an officer from the vice squad crowded into the tiny projection room.

'Where the hell did you get these?' Price thought he had seen everything, but the films he had witnessed in the last hour had been beyond belief.

Stein had looked sick. He gripped the arms of his chair tightly. 'Are these snuff movies, sir?'

For once, Morrow hadn't tried to put him down.

'In a way, I suppose they are,' he said. 'The thing is, we know that these are real.'

He turned to Price, answering his question. 'We've had four of them turn up over the last year, year and a half. We checked with other forces; similar numbers have turned up all over the country, some duplicated, and still others what look like salesman's samples. Made up of clips of other films, complete with titles and order numbers.' He shrugged. 'These things go in fashions and the open market follows the black market pretty damn closely. You remember a while back, the fuss that was made about the executions video? Well, we think that's pretty much what we have here, but with, shall we say, overtones that the straight version didn't have.'

Price felt sick. He glanced across at Beth Cooper. Her gaze was fixed carefully upon the screen and her features smoothed clear of all emotion. Tension showing in the fixed gaze and the way she held her pen, hard enough almost to break.

He switched back to watch the film. In the last two hours he had seen beheadings and amputations. Strangulation. A man dying in breathless agony, his lungs full of mustard gas, three-quarters of a century ago. Another, present-day in a small white room, an execution, Price guessed in some nameless American jail, the camera panning across the room to show the witnesses behind the plate-glass window.

Another scene, a kneeling man, the camera closing in on his face as realization dawned that the man dressed in combat gear and ski mask, with the gun in his hand, was for real. That he was going to die, here and now and without the hope of reprieve or mercy. A moment later and the man was dead. Brains and bone blasted across the lens as the camera came in close for the final shot. And intercut with it all, dancing shadow figures superimposed across the screen, the couples and singles and groups involved in sexual acts as varied and as starkly brutal as the many ways of dying Price had seen.

'It's this last scene I want you to look at.' Morrow's voice was oddly serious for him.

The final piece, a car, stationary upon a grassy hill, the camera panning across the scene then zooming in to show the courting couple in the back seat. Price felt every muscle tighten in anticipation and from across the room he heard Beth Cooper gasp. He wanted to look away, not to see it, but he found himself involved in the incident. Wrapped up in the plot in a way that both attracted and appalled. He couldn't look away even as he saw the flames begin to lick beneath the car. The flames begin to rise higher as the camera drew back far enough to show the entire scene. The couple in the car on the hill, the stillness of the summer's day.

'Why don't they move? Why don't they get out? Don't they know what's happening to them?' Stein's voice drawn thin with anguish. 'Why don't they get out?'

It seemed to last for ever, but Price knew that was just illusion. Less than half a minute had passed from gathering their first impression of the scene to the moment when the car exploded into flame. 'It was rigged,' he whispered. 'It was bloody rigged!'

He looked at Morrow who was nodding slowly. He'd

seen this before but the shock of it never left him and it showed now on his face.

Vaguely, Price was aware of Stein pushing himself from his chair and running from the room. Price's gaze was fixed upon the television screen as through the smoke he glimpsed the bodies burning up inside.

Chapter Thirty-Two

4 p.m.

Jake was editing his new film, the first section of the plotline already put together by actors, of a young man being kidnapped. In the film, he was hitching along a lonely road. It was night time, but there was enough light to catch the blond of his hair. He was quite tall, slender, dressed in the ubiquitous blue jeans and a dark top.

A car pulled up just ahead of him and he began to run towards it, then, when he reached the car and bent to look inside, it became clear that something was not quite right. The young man began to back away, then to turn and try to run, but already two people had emerged from the car and grabbed him. Pinning his arms behind his back they bundled him inside.

Jake re-ran the sequence, checking to see that there were no clear shots of the blond one's face. He'd use the same actor later for the final sequences, and for the major sequences up to the middle of the film; the face of the man he had down in the basement would be either covered or filmed obliquely. It would be easy enough to substitute the head shots later.

The initial sequence, Jake decided, would do. It didn't have the stark tension he would have liked, the real fear factor, but then even the best actors couldn't substitute for the real thing, the genuine terror of someone who's trapped with no way out and a growing fear that they are going to die.

Jake skimmed through to the later sequences, classic S & M skin shots, unremarkable but sound enough. The young man from the kidnap scene was doing what he was good at now. Jake flicked back through the script and the rough storyboard that he had put together to organize his shots. According to the brief he'd been given, the young man abducted in the early scenes, after a period of torture and humiliation, would not just co-operate with his captor's sexual desires – but would actively participate. It was, Jake thought, unimaginative and a little old-fashioned these days. A new take on the rape victim that was really gasping for it, hardly artistically demanding or particularly stimulating. But it would sell, and who was Jake to argue with the demands of economics?

He had begun to cut what were for Jake the interesting scenes. Those with blondie in the basement. Jake didn't know the guy's name, he wasn't interested, though he was mildly surprised that the man hadn't volunteered it. Most people these days saw enough TV drama and police reconstructions to know that you should try to make direct contact with your captor's psyche. Make yourself real for them. A person, not just a piece of meat, though such distinction would have been wasted on Jake.

He ran the sequence he'd been working on, something he'd shot that morning. It would need tightening up, but he figured he had enough footage not to have to do another take.

He had the sound turned down; soundtracks would be dubbed on afterwards by someone who was better at the words than he was. Jake was purely an image man. He made a note that Blondie's voice would need to be dubbed too. In some ways he was a bit of a disappointment. Not enough reaction. Jake needed him to plead and scream a whole lot more.

4.15 p.m.

Flint was still trying to get to grips with Myers. The man seemed to have worked himself into a loop and nothing Myers could do would break him out of it.

'I have done nothing,' Myers said in answer to almost every question.

'How did you get those scratches, Mr Myers?'

'I have done nothing, Superintendent Flint.'

'Where were you last Thursday evening, Mr Myers? From about six o'clock. Were you home? We could bring your wife in perhaps. Ask her.'

'I have done nothing wrong, Superintendent Flint.'

'And these other occasions? You're a businessman, an engineering consultant, isn't it? You must keep records, an ordered man like yourself. Where were you on March the twenty-fifth of this year? On April the nineteenth? On July the seventeenth?'

'I have done nothing wrong, Superintendent Flint. Nothing at all.'

'That's not what your record shows. And these young women, Mr Myers.' He laid a series of photographs on the interview room desk. 'These badly beaten, frightened young women. Recognize any of them, do you? Or did they all look different before you tried to bash their brains out through their ears?'

Flint paused. Myers continued to regard him steadily. He was furious, Flint knew, but keeping himself well under control now.

'I have done nothing wrong,' he said again.

And so it went on. It was only when Flint told him that they were going to search his house that Myers showed any emotion.

'You have a right to be there, of course,' he said.

Phillip Myers' eyes flickered with resentment, but he answered calmly. 'I have done nothing wrong.'

4.15 p.m.

The two uniformed officers listened to Terry's version of events. Maria was sitting close by, quietly encouraging. 'I went into the room,' Terry said, 'and she was just lying there. I thought she might be asleep at first; coming in through the door I could see her feet propped up on a cushion on the end of the sofa. But then I could smell it.' He hesitated for a moment, looking up at Maria as though needing encouragement.

She nodded. 'Go on, you're doing fine.'

The boy continued, his voice low and artificially steady, sitting on Maria's couch with Sarah beside him, clasping his hand tightly. Maria and John facing him. She had dimmed the lights. Only a single table lamp, casting more shadow than illumination across the scene, like some Italian chiaroscuro painting, all depth and light with little in between.

'I could smell the booze,' Terry said, 'and the sick.' His lips twisted in a look of disgust. 'I knew she'd had a problem; we'd talked about it.' He looked up quickly at Maria as though again needing approval. 'Because of my mum, you know. I couldn't get her to talk to me. She said I wouldn't understand, but Theo never ever said that. She treated me . . . like I was important to her, you know. Like an equal.'

He hesitated, and they all waited. At last Maria said, 'The last time we spoke, you mentioned Theo and I had the impression this was a new friendship. It wasn't though, was it?'

Terry shook his head. 'Months ago,' he said. 'In the summer. I . . . I liked her, Dr Lucas. I really liked her. I didn't want anything to spoil it. And it's always been the same, every time I made a friend, somebody would interfere. Try and break it up.' He licked his lips nervously, fidgeted with Sarah's hand. 'I even told her about me, about my mum, about Nathan. I thought she'd hate me, but she didn't. I knew my mum would go up the wall if she found out, either about Theo or Sarah. She would have hated it; she always got so scared when I made friends in case they found out. But Theo listened the way you do, but she didn't judge me.'

'I've never judged you, Terry,' Maria said steadily. 'You know that.'

'Yeah. But you're paid not to. Theo just didn't.'

Maria nodded slowly, not bothering to correct him.

Terry had no idea that her involvement with him was voluntary; she'd always figured it would just add to the burden of guilt the boy already carried.

She said, 'So what did you do, Terry? What happened then?'

'I went in. I thought, if she'd been drinking then it would have to be something really bad to make her start again, so I thought . . . she'd been to see the doctor. I thought it must be bad news. I'd promised to come round before David got home and see how she'd got on.'

'The doctor?'

'Yeah, some specialist in London, not her own doctor. She'd been to him when she lived there. When she was still an actress.'

Maria exchanged a glance with John. Even David had claimed not to know of Theo's illness. Had she confided in Terry?

'This doctor, Terry, did Theo tell you his name, or what she was seeing him about?'

He shrugged. 'Abbot or something. I don't know really. She usually just called him the specialist. She said she had pain, here.' He touched his stomach. 'I thought she just meant an ulcer or something. My grandad had an ulcer. But she said it was more than that. She said she'd brought it on herself with the drinking and stuff. I told her that was stupid.'

He fell silent then, staring at the simulated flames on Maria's gas fire. She found herself wishing, not for the first time, that the fire was real. That would have been more comforting, somehow.

'What did you do, Terry, when you found her? What did you see?'

The boy shuddered as though suddenly cold. Sarah moved closer to him and gripped his hand tighter. 'Tell them, Terry,' she said gently. 'Tell it like you told me.'

He nodded. 'It was like the other time,' he said.

John glanced at Maria, his look questioning. Other time?

'When Nathan . . . when Nathan died. The pillow was over her face. I was so scared.' He was almost whispering now, his gaze fixed and staring. It had been like reliving a nightmare. He had reached out, he told them, not daring to get too close, afraid of seeing Theo's face, blue-lipped like the baby's had been. He had reached out with fingertips, grasped the corner of the pillow and tugged it aside. Theo had been lying there, her eyes half-open and her mouth gaping, and he had known, without going any closer, that she was dead.

'Then I ran away,' he said simply. 'If they'd found me there no one would believe I hadn't hurt her. Just like they didn't believe me about the baby. About Nathan.'

He raised his head, looked desperately at Maria. 'I'm sure I didn't do anything, Dr Lucas. But I'm scared. Sometimes people do things and then they don't remember, do they? One therapist I had, she said people shut things out they don't want to think about. She went over and over, trying to get me to say I'd shut it out. Killing Nathan. She kept telling me it would be all right. That all I had to do was say I was jealous of my baby brother and that I killed him. Then they could help me. She kept on at me and on at me and so did my mum and everyone else that in the end I didn't even know what I really remembered any more and what I thought I did. So what if they were right? What if they were and I don't remember? I need locking up if they were, don't I? Don't I?'

There was silence. John, new to this, not knowing how to respond; the possibility that for the first time he had a proper suspect for his friend's murder hadn't escaped him. He forced himself not to react. To reserve judgement until he had some more of the facts.

Maria paused, then, professional tone carefully in place, she began quietly. 'I don't know what happened, Terry . . .'

But Sarah, who had been silent through all of this, seized on something he had said.

'You saw the baby's face. You said you saw the baby's face.'

They all stared at her. Sarah reddened but carried on. 'That means you must have moved the pillow, but you told me, when the baby was found, it had the bumper pad over its face.'

Terry stared at her, his eyes horrified as though in that simple deduction she had just confirmed his guilt.

'So I killed him,' he whispered. 'I must have done.' He tried to get to his feet, to pull his hand away from hers, but she was yelling at him that she wasn't saying that.

'No, she isn't,' Maria said, realizing where Sarah was leading him. 'She means you saw the baby's face after he was dead. That maybe Nathan was dead even before you went into his room. That maybe you saw him, like you saw Theo and knew you had to move the bumper pad from his face. Even quite small children know about smothering. Maybe you moved it then. Saw him, dropped it back when you heard your mother coming.'

Terry was staring at her, his face a conflict of emotions. 'I don't know,' he whispered. 'I just don't know. Maybe it was like that and maybe it was just an accident, but what if I did kill Nathan? What if I saw his face because I'd lifted the cushion up just to make sure that he was dead?'

Chapter Thirty-Three

4.30 p.m.

Vinnie Vincenza, alias Brian Hammond, had made a big thing of remembering Mike.

'Things have been looking up for both of us since you went away,' he said. 'I don't think you'd even made it to sergeant then.'

'Just,' Mike informed him. 'I'd just received promotion. A lot of water's passed under since then, Vinnie. I hear business is good. You have a place out of town these days.'

Vinnie laughed. 'Just like the old days,' he said. 'Always up with the gossip. Yeah, I've got a little place out Malmesbury way, though the truth is I only make it down for the weekends.' He grinned. 'This is still where the action is.'

Mike took the pictures of Marion from his pocket and laid them with the magazine on the table.

'I'm told she's one of yours, Vinnie.'

Vinnie picked up the polaroids and flicked through them with an air of professional interest. 'She was,' he said. 'Not any more though; this is a tough business we're in. You've gotta be professional.'

'And Marion wasn't?'

Vinnie shrugged expansively. 'Didn't turn up for a shoot. You're letting a lot of people down if a girl fails to show, doesn't do a whole lot for a man's reputation, so I crossed her off my list.'

'Did she give any explanation?'

Vinnie's eyes flickered sideways for the merest instant, then met Mike's again. 'Never a word,' he said. 'I left her messages, told her to give me a call, but nothing. That's the way it goes sometimes.'

He shrugged again, more reflectively this time. 'It was a pity. She had just what it takes to make it. Right to the top.'

Mike let the unconscious use of past tense go. Vinnie wasn't going anywhere at the moment and he didn't want to scare him off. He had no doubt that Vinnie either knew Marion was dead or suspected it.

'Did she do work for anyone else?'

'A little glamour work, that sort of thing. But she had a regular job and wasn't into selling herself cheap.' He wrinkled his nose. 'Choosy, you know. What she's been doing since she left me, I've no idea . . .'

Mike nodded and got up to leave. There was a lead here, he could feel it, but push too hard now and he might lose what edge he had. Better to use the local force, they'd have the background info.

Vincenza was seeing him to the door. 'You haven't told me what this is all about?'

'No, I haven't, have I?'

'Aw, come on, Mike . . . OK, OK, always the tight one, weren't you? Well, if you happen to run across my girl, tell her the door's always open.'

'I thought you didn't give people a second chance.'

'You know Vinnie. Always a soft touch.'

Mike left him, walking purposefully back towards his car parked two streets away. He paused once out of sight and back-tracked carefully, waiting ten minutes in the shadows of an alleyway behind a small hotel. Vinnie didn't show. Any longer and he would attract far too much attention.

Reluctantly, Mike made his way back to his car and the long drive home.

Maria called him just after he'd left Vinnie's and told him about Dr Abbot.

'I've already looked him up in the register,' she said.

'OK, give me the address and I'll fit him in before I come back.'

5.30 p.m.

Price and Morrow had returned to the place where Marion O'Donnel had died. Their mood was sober; Morrow had driven and had only terrified Price once.

They had left the car parked near Silbury Hill and climbed through the wire, Morrow puffing with exertion by the time they reached the top.

Around them lay fields, brown with winter earth, flecked with the white of the chalky landscape.

'They used to play cricket up here at one time,' Morrow commented.

'God help anyone that hit a six.'

Price walked to the edge of the flat-topped hill, looking across towards the village of Avebury.

'What about Vincenza?' he said.

'No evidence he's anything more than a two-bit creep. And, according to what he told your boss, he sold the pictures on elsewhere.'

'But the magazine thinks they came direct from him.'

'Maybe he sold them twice, or rather, sold Marion. Whoever hired her would do their own pictures, I presume. Or video,' he added, thinking of the stuff they'd seen that afternoon.

Price looked away. 'Yeah, could be she was into more than the odd centrefold.'

He turned back to Charlie Morrow, who seemed to be staring at something moving in the grass.

'Do we believe Vincenza?'

Morrow shrugged. 'Best we can hope for is apply for a warrant to search his place at Malmesbury and both offices. Could take a bit of time unless we get something more definite. It's going to involve three separate forces and God alone knows how many sub-divisions.'

Whatever it was that had attracted Morrow must have moved. Morrow edged towards it.

'What have you spotted?'

'Rabbit,' Morrow told him.

'Can't we just buy dinner at the Lion?' Price asked plaintively.

Morrow laughed briefly and inched towards the little animal. 'Lot of them still have myxie round here. Pitiful it is.'

'Myxie?'

'Myxomatosis. Used it to control the population.'

'Sure, but I thought that was years ago.' He watched, fascinated as the big man inched towards the rabbit.

He'd picked up a large stone in his right hand. The animal didn't move.

'You going to kill it?' He could see the animal clearly now. Milky eyes, unable to stand and with patches of fur hanging from its body. 'Christ,' he said.

Morrow brought the stone down squarely on the creature's head, then got back to his feet again and wiped his fingers on a bunch of serviettes he'd filched from Mickey's place that morning.

Price looked away.

They didn't speak again until they had reached the car, then, to break the silence, Price said, 'Beth Cooper. Attached, is she?'

Morrow gave him a predatory grin.

5.45 p.m.

Theo Howard's London doctor had his surgery in a quiet square in St John's Wood, amazingly quiet after the bustle of King's Cross. Mike could hear the birds sing.

'Yes, I saw Theo last week,' Dr Abbot told him. 'I'd been seeing her for years, usually minor complaints, a little depression from time to time. I gave her a medical once a year, that sort of thing, but until this, Theo had rarely ever been ill.'

'You knew what was wrong with her? You did the diagnosis?'

'I suspected what was wrong with her. Theo . . . Theo drank perhaps rather more than she should have done over the years. It became very serious at one time, but she was a tough lady. She worked her way through it. When she came to me I thought at first it was liver damage purely alcohol-induced. I sent her for tests. She had a tumour on the posterior lobe. It was operable but we suspected there were secondaries.' He frowned. 'You see, she put off coming to me until the pain began to get very bad. It wasn't that she was afraid of the pain, or even of dying. But she didn't want to die. She told me that she had met someone. Someone very special. I believe that for the first time in her life, Theo Howard had fallen in love.'

The two men were silent for a moment, then Mike said, 'We found no medication in her house. I would have thought . . .'

'I gave her pain-killers, this time. She's refused them every time before and you know, Inspector, pain is a funny thing. Some people have a high threshold. I think Theo must have been one of them, but it would not have lasted for much longer. The disease was spreading and there was nothing any of us could do. If you found no medication, well, I don't know.'

As Mike was leaving the doctor said, 'There's another thing. It might be unimportant but . . . Theo said she wanted to leave something for Davy to remember her by. Pictures, I think she said. She didn't want him to think of her as she was going to be in the end. She wanted to leave him something special. I thought she meant one of these makeover portraits at first. You know, there are studios that specialize in those things. She thought that was really funny, I remember. She seemed very excited about the whole thing. Like a child. Said she had something far more special in mind.'

9.00 p.m.

Flint had news when Mike got back to Norwich. The first check on Voters had drawn a blank, then Bristol had sent through a list of other aliases their suspect had used.

'They were used in different offences,' the collator explained. 'He was done for kiting, passing forged cheques, about seven years ago. Bristol dug around for the names he used then and guess what?'

'You've got a match on Voters.'

'Might not be connected, of course. Max Harriman might be just that. But he fits the general time frame, came here two months before the first attack occurred and is A blood group.'

'We're bringing him in,' Flint confirmed.

The call came a few minutes later. No Harriman, but the landlady lived on the premises and had let them in.

'He's our man, guv,' the officer's voice broke up a little. 'The walls are plastered with stuff. There's pictures of Marion O'Donnel and another woman and also some young kid. And books of press clippings. Looks like the man's into souvenirs.'

'Then we wait for him to come back,' Flint said.

'No need, guv, we've got his workplace. The landlady

insisted on a reference for him before she took him on. He's working shifts, finishes at ten.'

Flint looked across at Mike. 'Croft,' he said. 'You want to do the honours?'

Chapter Thirty-Four

9 p.m.

Less than a street away from one another, it felt as though Terry and Sarah were at opposite ends of the earth. Terry, seated at the kitchen table, stared morosely out of the window, trying at least to look as if he was concentrating on his essay.

For the last two hours he had tried to work. His mother had been so busy pretending that this was just another normal day, that Terry felt compelled to do the same. She had been dusting and polishing and bleaching the already spotless flat, filling the air with the stink of cleaning fluid and the atmosphere of angry busyness until Terry felt he could take no more.

His mind was full of questions that he couldn't ask her. Worries that he couldn't voice. He tried hard to write something sensible, but the essay he was writing seemed so far from any of the problems racing through his mind that he couldn't concentrate.

What if they decided it was him? What if they sent him away, to prison, to a young offenders' centre? To some secure psychiatric unit, locked up with the loonies.

He wasn't mad, he wasn't. He wasn't guilty either, he was sure of that . . . wasn't he?

Over and over again Terry ran through the twin events in his mind as if the two were linked, superimposed one against the other. A mess of images and impressions that merged and flowed and interrupted one another until he could no longer separate them out. Theo's face, Nathan's face. The fear he felt when he heard his mother coming.

Angrily, he tried to drag his thoughts back to Lenny's problems in *Of Mice and Men*. His hand wrote about the prejudice that Lenny suffered, the bright hot sunlight and the dim-lit barn and the woman taunting him, pushing him too far. In his mind, Lenny and he became one. The misunderstood. The odd one. Lenny, killing. Terry, killing. Lenny not understanding. Terry not knowing. His mind worrying at the problem like a puppy with a rag. His hand writing ordered words.

And outside, it was raining.

When Judith came into the kitchen he could bear it no longer.

'Did I do it?' he asked her, desperate for absolution. 'Did I kill Nathan?'

Sarah watched the rain lashing against her bedroom window. From this angle, she could see the back of Theo's house and, if she stretched on tiptoe, the rooftops of the taller houses at the end of the street where Terry lived.

She wished desperately that she could talk to him but knew her parents wouldn't hear of it. They had been by turns sympathetic and furious, still not understanding why she had gone off with 'that boy'.

They were madder than hell with her because she wouldn't tell them what Terry was running from. They knew it had something to do with Theo's death and

Sarah knew that her own mother and Terry's had talked, but she was certain they knew nothing about Nathan.

Sarah could just imagine the scenes that would be played if ever they found out.

Finally, she had been sent to her room and her mother had made a show of fastening the window locks in Sarah's room and taking away the key.

Sarah stared out through the wet glass, wishing, even, that she was back at school. Wondering when the blasted rain was ever going to stop.

9.35 p.m.

Jenkins' was an engineering company. Mike took three uniformed officers as back-up and went in quietly, but even so, the presence of one plain-clothes and three uniformed officers was not something to be easily hidden.

Other officers had been assigned to the three exits from the building.

'He's a lathe operator,' the night supervisor told them. 'Look, what the hell's going on here?'

'If you'll just point him out to us, sir,' Mike said quietly. Now they'd found their man they didn't want to lose him. He didn't feel it was the time for explanations.

'I'll take you through,' the man said.

Quite what alerted him, Mike was never afterwards quite sure. Events seemed to fall in upon one another in quick succession. One moment Mike was aware only of the noise of the machine shop, of having to shout over it to make himself heard as the supervisor pointed to the man in yellow ear-defenders working at the lathe down at the far end.

Then the man turned and saw them and he was running.

He had a head start, the full length of the engineering shop. Mike began to run, shouting to the officers who followed him to split up, try to head the man off. He didn't know if they had heard, but saw them move, hoped that someone would be in time. Trying to second-guess the route his suspect would be taking.

Beside him, the supervisor was gesturing. 'The fire escape. There's a fire escape that way.'

Had they anyone positioned there? Mike tried to visualize the layout of the building but was uncertain where the men outside would have taken up position.

He couldn't leave it to chance, he had to get to him before he made it to the door.

Around him was the roar of machinery, the sound of people shouting. Faces, gestures. Awareness that his leg, badly broken a few months before, was really not up to this. Then he saw the man ahead reaching for the fire escape door. Bursting through. The sudden rush of night air as the outside wind, damp with rain, surged in. Then Mike was through. Shouting ahead, hoping to make enough noise to alert whoever might be waiting below. One hand on the rail, one clutching his radio. Trying to predict where the fire escape might come down.

There was a sudden shout. The suspect dropped suddenly as though the ground had fallen out from beneath him. Mike looked down. The escape ended a good six feet from the ground.

'Damn!' He could see the man running down the back alley towards the main road. He expected to see officers come down the other way towards him, but at that moment there was no one. 'Where the hell is everyone? Suspect has reached the alleyway, repeat, reached the alleyway. Headed in the direction of Alden Street. Repeat Alden.'

Behind him one of the other officers crowded close and for a second Mike considered moving aside, letting him go ahead, but there was little room for manoeuvre. Mike swung himself out into empty air and dropped ungracefully into the alleyway. He could feel his leg protesting at the strain. Stumbled, then ran on, limping badly.

'You all right, sir?' The uniformed officer had landed beside him.

'Yes. Just get after the bastard.'

Then it was all over. At the end of the alleyway, Mike could see three officers, the suspect on the floor.

He steadied himself against the rough brick wall, then limped towards them, his leg and hip protesting every step of the way.

9.40 p.m.

Phillip Myers collected his things from the custody sergeant and walked out of the building without a word. He felt in his pockets. He had his front door key, a handkerchief, a little change. For the first time in years, he didn't even have enough to hire a cab.

He shivered. He didn't have his coat either.

There was a call-box on the corner of the road and Myers crossed over to it, oblivious of the traffic. He had enough change to call his wife.

'They've let me go. No charges,' he told her. 'Do you think, I mean, could you and Sarah come and fetch me home?'

10.35 p.m.

Mike had settled down to what was going to be a long night. A half-hour into the interview and Max Harriman was already causing problems. He wanted to confess to everything, he said. But wouldn't even let them know his real name.

'Names are unimportant, don't you think? They tell you nothing about the man. It's actions that are really important, not just names.'

Mike sighed. 'All right,' he said. 'For the moment, Harriman will do. Now, Mr Harriman, you were telling me about the woman that you met last night.'

An hour later they took a break in the interview. Flint was convinced that they could pin the whole series of attacks on their suspect, he seemed so willing to talk, to boast about what he had done. 'Forensics won't stand up to that, sir,' Mike reminded him. 'We know the first two attacks were carried out by someone with O group blood.'

241

Flint paced the room irritably. 'I know, I know,' he said. 'But God knows it's tempting anyway.' He brightened a little. 'We've cleared five of the eight girls – the path report on the latest victim just came in – and getting this one might well scare our other perp off our patch.'

'So he can become someone else's problem,' Mike said wryly.

'Oh, get real, Mike. You know his type as well as I do. He was someone else's problem before he was ours, and will carry on being someone's problem until either he gets caught or gets too old to get it up. People like him – for that matter, scum like him in there – they don't stop, they just go on and on until something puts a stop to them or they get too old for the chase.'

Mike fell silent. Then: 'What about Myers?' he said.

'What about him?' Flint shrugged. 'Dammit, Mike, if he wants to complain we'll feed it through the usual channels. It was a legitimate suspicion you had.'

'*I* had.'

Flint nodded. 'All right, *we* had. And I'm behind you on it all the way.'

10.45 p.m.

Jake had been making a delivery when he saw her and for a moment thought she looked like Marion. But no, at second glance, the similarity was superficial. Marion had a different way of moving, an indefinable quality that this girl didn't have.

He turned his back on her and locked the garage door.

This would be the last drop tonight. He rarely made deliveries himself these days but from time to time liked to check on security, in this case a strong-box hidden beneath the garage floor. They never knew when a delivery would be made. He demanded payment in advance, delivered the goods within ten days, but no set day and no set time. And no more than three issues to a set. He didn't believe in leaving merchandise in bulk, too much loss if someone got careless and the stuff was seized, and the price this stuff went for, he didn't have to deal in bulk.

He thought about Marion again as he got into his car. She could have been quite something if she hadn't got too stupid and threatened to give the game away. Talking of stupid, he had only himself to blame. First woman in a long time he'd allowed to get that close and it could have been an expensive mistake.

He wondered vaguely if Vinnie had any more like her on his list. The new editions would come out in a few weeks' time. Marion at her best, and no one would ask too many questions about where the pictures came from.

And later on, there would always be the new video.

Switching on his radio, he heard the first news of the other one's arrest. It was vague; talk of a police raid on an engineering firm and a suspect being interviewed about last night's murder and the previous attacks.

He was not surprised. Max was getting careless, always trying to impress. Jake had a feeling the man would try to cop for all the previous assaults, even Jake's score. He was that sort, liked to play the numbers game when, they both knew, Jake out-classed and out-scored him every time.

Jake turned the radio up, started the engine and drove away.

11.45 p.m.

The police photographer had finished at Harriman's flat and the cuttings books and pinned up clippings removed and brought to the police station.

Mike was told as soon as they came in. He took them to the interview room and lay the cuttings books out on the table in front of Harriman. There were eight in all, the last not yet complete.

Max looked at them but made no attempt to touch the books wrapped inside evidence bags.

'Are they yours, Mr Harriman?'

Max looked across at him and smiled. He had, Mike thought, a truly appealing, ingenuous smile that creased the corners of his eyes and lit his entire face. It was a strange thing to think about a possible murderer.

'I collected them,' Max told him. 'For posterity.'

'Posterity?'

Max nodded. 'You see, Inspector Croft, we've been making history here, and now,' that smile again, 'now you're a part of it too.'

Mike ignored the boast. 'These young women, Mr

Harriman. You were telling me about the attacks on these young women.'

Harriman nodded.

'We know you're not responsible for them all,' Mike went on. 'No, no we *know* you're not.' This as Max began to protest. 'There were two separate blood types you see. O and A. Yours is A, and, much as my boss would love to see this whole thing cleared up in one go, we know that someone else attacked two of those girls. You can't take credit for them all, Mr Harriman.'

Max Harriman smiled and he shrugged his shoulders as though conceding the point. 'I had a good teacher, Inspector Croft,' he said. 'He set a fine example for me to follow.'

Mike let the implication sink in. 'You know the other man?' he said.

Harriman merely smiled.

After leaving the police station, Davy had ridden the bus to its terminus before he'd even thought of what he had to do next.

Finally, he had walked back to Theo's house, but the police seal was still across the door, a reminder that they still did not know who had taken his Theo's life.

There was, he thought, nothing left for him here, but he had no idea of where to go or what to do.

Finally, he had taken a taxi to John Tynan's cottage and retrieved his car. Tynan wasn't there – Davy was relieved about that. John would have been full of more questions that Davy didn't know the answers to. Then he had begun to drive.

Close to midnight and he sat on the stones at the mouth of West Kennet Barrow. Uncertain what had brought him here, but glad that he had come.

Inside, someone had lit candles and their faint glow lit the barrow forecourt. It was beginning to rain once more, a slow, steady drizzle that would soak him to the skin.

Davy knew that he should move and go back to his car, but the rain continued to fall and Davy sat, his hair dripping water down on to his face. Davy no longer knew what was rain and what was tears.

11.50 p.m.

Terry had taken a break from work. He watched as his mother buttered bread for sandwiches and made tea. She had barely spoken to him all day and when she had it had been with that false brightness that Terry hated. That 'Let's just forget everything and get on with life' brightness that had nothing to do with the way either of them was feeling.

'Can I go to the funeral?' Terry asked. The question had come out of the blue, taking even himself by surprise. He had been thinking about it off and on all day. Theo's funeral. He knew that he wanted to go.

His mother ignored the question. 'Do you want pickle with this?' she asked him. 'Or mayonnaise?'

'I asked you something,' Terry said. 'I want to go, Mum. I want to go to Theo's funeral.'

The knife stopped moving. His mother halted what she was doing, her hands limp on the kitchen counter.

'Do you honestly think anyone will want you there?' she said, her voice hoarse with emotion. 'She'll have family, friends. What makes you think they'll even want you there?'

Terry stared at her, hurt and angry. 'I was her friend, Mum.'

His mother turned on him. She slammed the knife down on the counter and whirled around to face him, the tension and strain of the weekend suddenly breaking over her.

'Your friend,' she hissed, 'that woman was your friend, was she? You think she'd have been your friend if she'd known about you? Known what they said about you. Known all the gossip we've been trying to protect you from. Me and your grandad and everyone?' She stopped suddenly, wringing her hands in desperation. 'You can't have friends like that, Terry, love. People like that who might talk and not understand you. I wanted you to understand that for yourself, not have to do everything for you. You have to grow up, Terry, realize that however much you try, however much either of us try, it can't be normal and easy and all the things I know you want. Life's not like that, Terry. It never was.'

Terry stared at her. 'You knew about Theo?' he said. 'Mum, did you know about Theo?'

'Of course I knew. Not because you told me either.

Always creeping around the way you do, keeping things from me, but I knew about her and about that girl.'

'You followed me?' Terry was incredulous. He thought he had been so careful.

'I was going to tell her,' Judith said, her voice falling almost to a whisper. 'Tell her to keep away from you. I didn't want you hurt if ever she should find out.'

Terry shook his head. 'Theo did know,' he said. 'I told her. I told her about the night Nathan died and about how everybody thought I might have done it and how you started drinking and all the things you never wanted to talk to me about. I told Theo, Mum, because I knew she'd listen to me and help me sort out what I really felt and what I thought and what I couldn't understand. And she did. She didn't hate me and she didn't think I was some kind of creep. And you know what she said? She said she didn't believe I could have done it. She said that accidents happen and that maybe the padding just wasn't tied up right. And something else. She said I was still the person she had known before I told her and it wasn't her way to hate someone just for being honest about what had happened to them. That made me feel good. Better than all the secrets and all the . . . everything.'

He'd run out of words, he could see his mother's face, cold and white with anger. 'After all I've tried to do for you,' she said. 'All I've tried to protect you from.'

She walked unsteadily to the table, pulled out a chair and sat down.

'I love you, Terry,' she said softly. 'You know that, don't you? I really love you, kid.'

'Oh Jesus, yes I know you do.' He went over and stood beside her, pulling her close to him, holding her tightly as though he was the adult and she was the child.

Tuesday,
20 December

Chapter Thirty-Five

12.45 a.m.

Terry crept downstairs to the hallway. It was well after midnight, but he couldn't think of what else to do. His mother had been so odd, talking little all evening and when she had spoken it had seemed like nonsense.

At last, she had seemed to make up her mind about something and had told him to call Maria Lucas.

'But it's so late,' Terry had objected. But she had insisted.

Maria listened to what he had to say. 'All right,' she said finally, reacting more to the distress in his voice than to his confused words. 'I'll be there in about an hour. You just hold on till then.'

John had spent the evening with her and stayed over, as he'd drunk a little too much wine. She'd put him up in one of the rooms they kept for the overnight staff.

She padded along the hallway and tapped lightly on the door, then went in.

'John,' she said. 'I've just had a call from Terry, he seems pretty upset, something about his mum. I need you to go with me.'

2 *a.m.*

'I only went to talk to her,' Judith said softly. 'I knew about you and that woman. I'd seen you talking to her. Believe me, Terry, all I wanted to do was talk to her. Tell her she wasn't wanted. That we didn't need her kind. I went into the house. I'd tried knocking on the door but there was no reply, but I knew she was in there. When I'd come home I'd seen her go inside. So I tried the door.'

She paused, looking up at Terry, fixing him with an intense gaze. 'I went into the room and I saw her lying there. Blind drunk and I thought, this is the woman who my son looks up to. The woman he'd rather spend time with than me. This disgusting drunk, lying there in her own stink.'

Terry stared at his mother. 'You killed her?' he whispered. 'You killed Theo?'

Judith nodded slowly. 'It didn't take much, really, it was so easy. I couldn't stand to think of her with you.'

'And Nathan?' Terry whispered.

Judith looked away.

'So what happens now?' Terry asked as his mother was led away. He looked exhausted, Maria thought. Utterly spent.

'For tonight,' John said, 'I can offer you a place to stay. Tomorrow, we can talk it through, decide what's best.'

Terry nodded. All he really wanted to do now was sleep. His head just couldn't get around it all.

'Do you think she did that too?' he whispered softly. 'Do you think she killed Nathan?'

Maria clasped his hand gently. 'I don't know, Terry,' she said, meeting John's eyes. 'I just don't know.'

3 a.m.

Harriman was getting bored. He had wanted to take Mike through his cuttings books, and for a while Mike had listened carefully to all he had to say. It had become clear, though, that it was not what this stupid policeman wanted right then. He had failed to see the significance of it all.

'Vinnie Vincenza,' Mike repeated patiently. 'You were telling me about Vincenza.'

Max sighed, turning his gaze to the ceiling. 'Vincenza sells pictures,' he said. 'He's a little man, with little ideas, and will never be any more than that.'

'This woman.' Mike turned the centrefold picture of Marianne back to face Max and laid the polaroids that Davy had taken beside it. 'This woman,' he repeated. 'Vinnie Vincenza sold her pictures to this film-maker. This Jake Bowen you told me about?'

Jake's name caught Max's attention once again and he smiled sweetly at Mike.

'Jake is not a little man,' he said. 'Not like Vincenza. Jake is a maestro.' He reached out again for one of the cuttings books. 'It started with one little film, all those years ago. We were children then, you know, just children, but the vision was there . . .'

Jake was editing film, making the cuts to the closing sequences.

Marion's last film was ready for distribution now and he was pleased with it. He'd included something very special in the final run. Those last seconds of film, showing the car well ablaze, Jake had taken with a long lens. He had let his eye rest on the flames, the black smoke billowing through the open window and into the damp air, and then that final moment he had hardly dared to hope would come about when for an instant the smoke had cleared and Jake had seen her face.

Jake sat back and reviewed the end of the kidnap film. He'd finished with Blondie in the cellar, disposed of him earlier with a single shot at point-blank range. Jake had let the blond one watch the preparations. Covering the floor and walls with plastic sheet to make the cleaning up easier. Jake had taken time to explain it to him. How it would be in the end, and had finally got the screams of fear that had eluded him so far.

In the final analysis it had turned out well.

Jake's mind turned briefly from the job in hand to wonder what Max was telling the police.

Chapter Thirty-Six

8.30 a.m.

They had little sleep that night. Terry had collapsed straight away, but had been awake and restless again an hour later and the adults had fared no better. By the time Mike arrived along with the morning post, they were sitting at the breakfast table feeling very sorry for themselves and Maria knew she had a busy day ahead of her.

'My mum,' Terry began. 'She all right?'

Mike nodded slowly. 'Your mum was taken to the hospital last night, Terry. We got the doctor in to see her and they decided she'd be better off there.'

'Which one?' Terry asked him. He swallowed hard. 'I mean, can I see her?'

'I'll find out what I can this morning. I promise you.'

Terry nodded and fell silent, stirring his tea. Mike began to speak again, wondering what to say to the boy, but Maria shook her head and he left well alone.

'What's in the post?' she said.

John was reading something, his face drawn and pale. 'John?'

'It's from Theo, my dear. Written on the day she died.' He picked up the padded envelope and glanced at the postmark. 'Though the package wasn't posted until Friday.' He reached inside the envelope. Inside was a video. John laid it on the table.

'It's for David,' he said. 'A final gift. She says she

made this film over thirty years ago when she was just starting out and needed money. She says she wants me to keep it, give it to Davy when . . .' He paused, then read on:

'But I've never regretted it, John. The girl I starred with went on to take far bigger roles than I did. You might recognize the face. In those days, we all seemed to do at least one blue film. It paid the rent and I've never felt ashamed or that I needed to apologize.

'When I knew that I didn't have long left, I felt so dreadful, John. Not because death frightens me. It never has. Life has always been the hard bit. But there was Davy and I loved him so much, you know. I always intended to finish things myself, before the pain got too bad. I didn't want Davy suffering. I wanted him to know me, to remember me, not as I knew I would be in the last days and weeks, but when I was young and vibrant and just starting out.

'There was a young woman Davy used to know. She'd called a few times and, well, you know how it is, we'd got talking. She told me about a friend of Davy's who could help me and so I called his friend, Mr Vincenza.'

'His friend,' John laughed harshly.

'And he helped me to make this happen and he had the film transferred on to video for me.'

'And this is it,' John said, fingering the video as though he had a precious relic lying on the table.

8.30 a.m.

Jake woke early, feeling relaxed and content with the world. He had some holiday due to him from his regular job and felt that now would be a good time to take it. Escape from the winter and get some sun. He made a mental note to book the time off later that day.

He'd disposed of Blondie's body. Jake had been undecided as to what to do with him, but finally decided to take him back where he'd found him. Leave him in the alleyway at the side of the nightclub. Occasionally, but only occasionally, the love of risk got the better of him.

11 a.m.

Morrow led the way, Stein and Price in tow, following the instructions given on Vincenza's tape.

The search warrant had been issued early. The Vincenza house was impressive. Mock Tudor, complete with swimming-pool and billiard-room. Officers combed the house and grounds but Morrow was going straight for the jugular.

The store room backed on to the billiard-room. A second safe had been sunk into the floor beneath false boards.

Vincenza had the combination but claimed he had no knowledge of what had been left inside. He never looked, he said. His fear of the film-maker he called Bowen was tangible even through the medium of tape.

Morrow knelt and lifted the boards, took the paper from his pocket and began to turn the dial.

The doorway was narrow. Price leaned against the frame, watching. Stein waited just outside.

'Right, this is it, boys,' Morrow said. He sat back on his heels, his heavy body sagging. Then reached down and pulled the door.

A sheet of flame shot through the narrow room and caught Morrow with full force. Threw Price off his feet and backward into the billiard-room. He heard his own voice, screaming, then shouting Charlie Morrow's name.

Pulling himself to his feet, he struggled forward. The drapes had caught and cardboard boxes piled against the wall. In the centre of the room something still living writhed and fought in agony. Price could hardly breathe. Fire in his lungs, they burned so much. He tried to throw himself towards the thing that burned to pull it free before the fire caught even fiercer hold, but his body didn't want to move and everything seemed to be so slow.

Somehow, he grabbed Charlie Morrow's arm, screaming as the fire bit naked hands. Beside him, Stein had hold of him the other side and they dragged the big man from the room. Then Price fell to the floor, retching, hardly able to breathe, dimly aware that there were others now, helping him outside.

It was rigged, the voice whispered in his head. It was bloody rigged.

11.25 p.m.

At a Travel Inn on the M25 Mr John Phillips checked in for the night. The news was full of it. The arrest of the Norwich rapist. The big copper who'd been blown up in the raid on Vincenza's house, they didn't know if he would live or die, it said.

Jake Bowen smiled. Pity he wasn't there, he thought. It would have made fantastic film.

FINAL FRAME
by Jane Adams

What follows here are the opening scenes to Jane Adams' new novel, *Final Frame*, a direct sequel to *Fade to Grey*.

It is available in hardback from Macmillan, priced £16.99.

Prologue

They had been forced to leave the car parked at the head of the lane and carry their equipment along the narrow track.

From the top of the hill they got a view across the valley for the first time, the high hedges either side of the road having blocked any sight of the landscape as they had driven up. It was a beautiful but claustrophobic place.

Liz pointed across to the opposite rise. 'That's the farm where we asked directions. See, it's marked on the map and this' – she nodded towards the house at the side of the lane – 'must be the Jenkins' place.'

Macey nodded, swinging the camera bag across his shoulder. 'Through there,' he said, pointing to a narrow opening between the trees.

Neither spoke as they pushed their way along what was little more than a rabbit track through a tangle of trees and across a plank bridge over a tiny stream. They reached the second stile, beyond which was forestry commision land. Here, they both paused. Liz exchanged a glance with Macey; there was no need for words. The tip-off had come in a couple of hours before. If this was for real then they had a very shrewd idea of who had brought them to this place and suddenly, being here, just the two of them, didn't seem too bright.

'Maybe we should have waited for the police,' Liz suggested tentatively.

Macey shook his head. 'And have them get here to find it's all a wind-up?'

Liz gave him a wry look. Macey didn't believe the hoax theory any more than she did. He just wanted to be there first before the arrival of the local police pushed them back behind the usual barriers. Macey had followed every angle of this business as it had been reported in the nationals and now this had happened on his home ground. If it was for real, this could be *it* for Macey. His break into the big time.

Macey made the first move, handing his equipment to Liz while he eased himself over the stile, then helping her across. Behind them, the mixed woodland they had left was alive with the noise and rustling of wildlife. Here, in this dimly lit conifer plantation, there was an uncanny stillness.

'I don't like this place,' Liz whispered, expecting one of Macey's usual ascerbic rejoinders. But for once the big man was silent.

They looked around. Behind them, the hill continued to rise, densely planted and very dark. The path itself was wider than it had been but dropped off to the right, falling down the hill into a steep gully.

Below, in the gully, there was only a chaos of fallen trees and deeply channelled earth eroded by the winter rains. It was so quiet. All around the rustling and busyness and the call of birds continued as it had since they had entered the wood, but here, within a rough circle of dying trees, there was no sound. Liz looked again at the sketch map. This was definitely the place.

She and Macey began to scramble down. It took all of their attention just to keep their footing and protect their camera equipment from being slammed against the rough ground and exposed roots. They did not see it until the trees thinned and the scene was suddenly there, exposed in all its terrible beauty.

The body lay, naked, on a rough bed of fallen branches and fresh flowers. All around, on every low branch, every niche that could be used, stood tiny candles, their white stems gleaming in the flickering light.

Mike turned away from the crime scene and walked along the head of the gully and towards the second stile. Beyond that, the path broadened out, allowing an avenue of sunlight to break through between the tall trees. He climbed over the stile, relieved to get out of the darkness and into the warmth of the early summer's day. The sudden heat on his back enough to persuade him out of his jacket.

He held a large scale OS map in his hand and referred to it now. Further along, the path apparently turned into a gated road leading back towards Honiton.

Which way had Jake Bowen come in? Mike wondered. The narrow road and rabbit path that Macey and Liz Thompson had taken or this other road? And had the woman been alive when he brought her here?

Mike leaned heavily against the fence post next to the stile. His back in shadow, facing into the sun. This last six or seven months Mike felt as though he's done nothing but live and breathe Jake Bowen, especially the last eight weeks since he'd been seconded to this operation along with practically anyone who'd ever had dealings with the killer. Mike had found himself dragged over half the country, chasing one short-lived lead after another, finally fetching up here. The middle of nowhere and a long way from home.

'Penny for them?'

Mike turned with a slight smile. 'Not worth it, sir. I was trying to work out the last time I had a weekend off.'

Chief Superintendent Mark Peterson returned the smile. 'Probably about the same time I did,' he said. 'And it's not likely to be this weekend either.'

'No. I'd arranged for Maria to come down.'

'Ah. I'll tell our man to improve his timing.' He paused for a moment. 'Look, Mike, get your lady to come anyway. Unless something breaks fast you'll be able to wangle a couple of hours free.'

'Thanks. I'll do that.'

Peterson leaned against the fence and gazed out, eyes squinting, into the sunny space between the trees.

'I've got someone walking in from the other end, looking for tyre tracks, anything out of the ordinary.'

'Doubt they'll find anything. Last two weeks have been too damned dry. I asked one of the locals,' Mike added by way of explanation.

'You been down there yet?' Peterson gestured towards the gully.

'Briefly. I came back up top, let the photographer and

SOCO do their bit. There's enough bodies down there as
it is.'

Peterson laughed gruffly at the unintended humour.
'We'd better get back and join them,' he said. 'They've
just warned me the surgeon's on his way.'

A sound overhead made both men look up sharply. A
squirrel, its tail flying out behind it as it leapt between
trees. Peterson laughed again with relief. 'You know,
Mike, I'm not a man given to all that much imagination,
but if when we find this bugger, he's got hooves and a
forked tip in his tail, I'm not going to be surprised.'

A shout from behind them in the gully told them that
the police surgeon had arrived. Mike eased himself over
the stile and they made their way back along the path.
Peterson's comment had come as no surprise, everyone
was as jumpy as hell. He glanced sideways. The man's
rather round face, reddened by too much sun, had gained
lines these last weeks. Peterson was a robust man. Taller
than Mike's six two and heavier, but the strain of the
Bowen hunt was beginning to tell on him and recently
he seemed to have shrunk in on himself.

Some fifteen years older than Mike, Peterson was a
career copper who'd made it up through the ranks. His
present title, Chief Super, was being phased out in one
of the 'reforms' sweeping through the service and men
like Peterson, who seemed to belong to another time,
were finding it hard to make their way in the new order.

Promoted sideways to head up 'Operation Final
Frame' – Mike wondered who made these things up –
this was likely to be the last thing he'd see through before
he retired.

DI Mike Croft had grown to like and respect the man a great deal and knew it was an opinion largely shared by the rest of the team. Under other circumstances, Mike would have enjoyed working with this large, bluff man with the overgrown moustache. Under these circumstances, Mike wished himself anywhere but here.

It was not an easy scramble down into the gully. Tree roots reaching from the dry ground and hard, rutted furrows cut by the last heavy rains then dried by the summer heat, threatened to undermine every step. The scene, when they reached bottom, was pretty much as Macey and Liz had viewed it. It looked, thought Mike, like a scene from a low-budget horror flick, but this was real. The woman, her long hair carefully combed out across the bed of flowers on which she lay, her hands folded prayerfully between her breasts and the long thin line of blood that had flowed from the artery in the girl's throat down across the flowers. White roses stained a rusty brown as it had dried.

'Bled her like a bloody pig,' Peterson said.

All Pan Books are available at your local bookshop or newsagent, or can be ordered direct from the publisher. Indicate the number of copies required and fill in the form below.

Send to: Macmillan General Books C.S.
              Book Service By Post
              PO Box 29, Douglas I-O-M
              IM99 1BQ

or phone: 01624 675137, quoting title, author and credit card number.

or fax: 01624 670923, quoting title, author, and credit card number.

or Internet: http://www.bookpost.co.uk

Please enclose a remittance* to the value of the cover price plus 75 pence per book for post and packing. Overseas customers please allow £1.00 per copy for post and packing.

*Payment may be made in sterling by UK personal cheque, Eurocheque, postal order, sterling draft or international money order, made payable to Book Service By Post.

Alternatively by Access/Visa/MasterCard

Card No.

Expiry Date

Signature   _____

Applicable only in the UK and BFPO addresses.

While every effort is made to keep prices low, it is sometimes necessary to increase prices at short notice. Pan Books reserve the right to show on covers and charge new retail prices which may differ from those advertised in the text or elsewhere.

NAME AND ADDRESS IN BLOCK CAPITAL LETTERS PLEASE

Name _____

Address _____

_____

_____

_____

8/95

Please allow 28 days for delivery.
Please tick box if you do not wish to receive any additional information. ☐